LAUREL

"CONCISE, AFFECTING, AND HIGHLY ORIGINAL. . . .
Readers will not be disappointed. . . . *Mrs. Caliban* never makes its
points head-on, never strays from its intriguing confusions, never
beats us over the head with meaning, but somehow we are moved."
—*The New York Times Book Review*

"*Mrs. Caliban* has the creeping effect of a story read at bedtime.
When it's over, the characters live on in that mental niche that is
somewhere between sleep and wakefulness."
—*People* magazine

"RACHEL INGALLS COULD BECOME THE [NEXT]
BARBARA PYM. . . . By turns droll and erotic most of the way,
Mrs. Caliban ends in a blaze of Shakespearean evil."
—*The Atlantic*

"Nothing I've read since Gogol's 'The Nose' and 'The Overcoat'
has offered such a satisfying blend of the fantastic and the quotidian,
the satiric and the sentimental . . . a remarkable tour de force."
—*The Sun* (Baltimore)

"As odd and disconcerting as Thomas Pynchon's great short novel
The Crying of Lot 49."
—*Sunday Journal* (Providence)

"SO FULL OF SURPRISES, everyone I know who's read it has
done so in one sitting. . . . *Mrs. Caliban* deserves a sit-down, settle-in,
old-fashioned evening-to-midnight read."
—*Seattle Weekly*

"SUPERB. . . . It's a masterfully written fable for our particular
time, both topical and provocative in its evocation and exploration
of late-20th-century life and expectations."
—*Houston Chronicle*

8/89

MRS. CALIBAN
RACHEL INGALLS

LAUREL

A LAUREL TRADE PAPERBACK
Published by
Dell Publishing Co., Inc.
1 Dag Hammarskjold Plaza
New York, New York 10017

Mrs. Caliban first published in Great Britain by Faber and Faber Limited

Laurel ® TM 674623, Dell Publishing Co., Inc.

ISBN: 0-440-50003-6

Reprinted by arrangement with Harvard Common Press and Gambit

Printed in the United States of America

February 1988

10 9 8 7 6 5 4 3 2 1

W

$\mathcal{F}$red forgot three things in a row before he reached the front door on his way to work. Then he remembered that he had wanted to take the paper with him. Dorothy didn't bother to say that she hadn't finished with it yet herself. She just went back and brought it to him. He dithered for a few more minutes, patting his pockets and wondering whether he ought to take an umbrella. She told him the answers to all his questions and slipped in several more of her own: would he need the umbrella if he had the car, did he really think it felt like rain? If his car had that funny noise, couldn't he take the bus instead, and had he found the other umbrella yet? It must be at the office somewhere; it was a nice telescoping one and she suggested that someone else had walked off with it.

They had run through a similar litany many times before. It was almost as though Fred needed the set words of this ritual to keep him steady at the beginning of days which held some test for him, something he was nervous about.

"I may be back late tonight," he said. "Something about—I don't know yet, but I'll call from the office. O.K.?"

"Sure. All right."

She stood by the door while he went out and down the front walk. He didn't look back. And, of course, he hadn't kissed her goodbye for years. This was the same way that affair of his with the publicity girl had started: staying late at the office. Maybe. Or perhaps it was genuine, but she couldn't tell anything about him any longer.

She made the beds, vacuumed, washed and dressed, and was at the kitchen sink doing the dishes when she looked over at the radio and thought about turning it on. It was a large, dark brown old-fashioned set, the kind that looked like a 1930's Gothic cathedral.

For the past three weeks she had been hearing things on the programmes that couldn't possibly be real. The first time was during a commercial for cake-mix and the woman's voice had said in a perfectly ordinary tone (just like the rest of the ad), "Don't worry, Dorothy, you'll have another baby all right. All you need to do is relax and stop worrying about it. It's guaranteed." And then the voice had gone straight back into the cake-mix that couldn't fail.

She hadn't thought she was going crazy, not straight away. She believed it was just her own thoughts forcing themselves into the low-pitched sounds and their insistent rhythm. But, the next day she had heard a story on a news programme about a chicken that could play the violin—"the Heifetz of the hen-coops", the bird had been called—and later found out through friends that that item had not been heard by other people who had evidently been tuned in to the same spot on the dial.

Well, then. It was an old radio, after all. A very old radio. Surely it was possible that the sound waves were

getting mixed up, or something like that. Some kind of
static or interference which made no particular irritating noise but just cut in and blended with the general
tone of the programme it collided with. Dorothy did
not set the sound very high, since she only wanted the
noise to be in the background, to keep her from brood-
ing but not from thinking. She had now taken to turning the sound up higher when she heard something
unusual, and she honestly couldn't see where the
original programme was cut or faded and the other one
joined in. The voices sounded precisely similar, only the
tone was somehow altered and meant specially for her.

She still didn't think she was going crazy. However,
she was now apprehensive about turning the machine
on. Once the talk or music began, she became happy
and relaxed. Only at the moments when she realized
that one of the special announcements was in progress,
would she feel a thrill of expectation and mild alarm.
What she did not want to hear was anything more
about having a baby, or about her and Fred, and their
marriage. So far, that first announcement had been
the only personal one. Still, there might be others. She
had not told anyone about hearing them, least of all
Fred. Of course not.

She stood with one hand on the faucet and looked
across to the radio. This was the hour when she could
tune in to the foreign stations and hear classical music
without static.

She crossed to the radio and switched it on, catching
a symphony in the middle of an expanding ladder of
big chords. She began to hum and turned on the water
at the sink. The orchestra soared and crashed its way

to a finale which was going to be really tremendous—
there were even introductory drum-rolls—and then it
all seemed to dim off and a voice, even and distinct,
said:

*Ladies and gentlemen, we interrupt this programme
to make the following announcement to all citizens in
the area. Early this morning, keepers at the Jefferson
Institute for Oceanographic Research were attacked
by a creature captured six months ago by Professor
William Dexter on his South American expedition.
The creature, known to the popular press by its nick-
name "Aquarius the Monsterman", appears from
intensive scientific analysis to be a giant lizard-like
animal capable of living both underwater and on dry
land for extended periods. It is also highly dangerous,
as this morning's tragic events all too clearly bear
witness, for two of the Institute's employees, keeper
John Kelsoe and Dr Dennis Wachter, were found dead
and horribly mutilated near the animal's empty cage.
When Aquarius was first installed in the Institute, it
was hoped that he might prove an attraction for
students from all over the country, but the scientists
assigned to study his habits agreed that there was a
great danger that contact with large numbers of people
might expose him to contagious diseases which,
although harmless to the human race, might be fatal
to his mysteriously different physiology. And, they
added, he was possessed of incredible strength and
should be considered extremely dangerous, especially if
roused to one of his furies. This warning has now proved
tragically correct, as only the loved-ones of these two
men can know—these two who died while loyally and*

*bravely carrying out the rigorous duties of searchers
after knowledge. We underline this warning to everyone in the area: this animal is violent and should on
no account be approached. If you see him, phone
the police immediately. Repeat: the monsterman is
dangerous.*

For a moment, Dorothy had thought that the bulletin about Aquarius was one of her special announcements. But it couldn't be. Her special voices never
lasted long and had a soft, close, dreamlike quality,
heard in the ear as though they emanated from the
organ itself instead of outside it. This tirade had been
spoken in the usual emotionally heightened drone of
the salesman-advertiser.

If Scotty had lived, she would now be telephoning
to the school to let them know that she'd be picking him
up herself in the afternoon on account of the warning.
Even though he would be a grown boy by now; how
old? He had died under an ordinary anaesthetic given
before a simple appendectomy, and afterwards all anyone could say in explanation was "individual reaction",
"unsuspected allergy" and "drug sensitivity". And, a
few months later, she lost the baby. That was the point
where things began to change with Fred. The first
blow had stunned them both, but the second had
turned them away from each other. Each subtly blamed
the other while feeling resentment, fury and guilt at
the idea that a similar unjust censure was radiating
from the opposite side. Then, it became easier to sweep
everything under the carpet; they were too exhausted
to do anything else. And so it went on: silences,
separateness, the despair of thinking out conversations

that they knew would be hopeless. Long before he was unfaithful, he decided on the single beds. They were both having trouble sleeping and would wake at different times. And, after all, it wasn't as though for the moment they were making any use of being in the same bed. She knew it was the end when he said that, but she didn't have the strength to do anything about it. He couldn't have had much strength either, or they would have been divorced by now. Sweep everything under the rug for long enough, and you have to move right out of the house.

At ten past eleven the telephone rang and Fred told her that the car—his famous, lovingly-cared-for old car —had broken down again, that he was going to be late, and that he might be bringing someone back for supper. Just a snack, because they had to talk something over.

"Find out if he's a vegetarian or some kind of health-food freak, will you?" Dorothy said. "I'm not serving a steak to somebody who's going to scream his magic mantra at me."

"No, he isn't. Just anything. Beer and sandwiches."

"Oh no, I'll give you something hot. But if you don't say right now what you want me to get in, it's going to be spaghetti Bolognese and a salad. And ice cream."

"That sounds fine. See you," he said, and hung up, long before she had expected him to. It left her feeling slightly upset and annoyed, first with him and then with herself.

She changed into her leotard and did her exercises in the spare bedroom. She did the regular dance exercises, not the ones you were supposed to do just to keep yourself in shape. She started without music and then brought the radio in and turned it on.

She liked being in the guest room, which had never held a guest. It was really meant for storing trunks or furniture. The one they used for guests was much larger. She had painted this one herself and put up curtains. There was already a bed, and a bathroom next door. Originally they had thought it would be a playroom for the children, which would have been convenient, since it was on the ground floor. Two or three of Scotty's toys were still in the bottom drawer of one of the dressers. Fred wouldn't go near the place. He probably thought it was still full of garden furniture and the croquet set and other things that Dorothy had moved when Mr Mendoza built the outdoor shed for them.

She was in the middle of what she thought of as a Swan Lake gesture when the music slowed down and a low voice from the radio said very faintly so that she could only just make out the words: "It's all right, Dorothy. It's going to be all right."

She stood up straight and found that she was covered with sweat. The music ran on as it had been before. She went into the bathroom and stripped, stood under a short burst of water from the shower, changed her clothes, washed the sweat out of the leotard and hung it over the curtain rail.

She drove in to town and bought some mushrooms and meat and cheese. In the supermarket someone took a flying run at her shopping wagon and crashed into her. It was her friend Estelle, who said, "O.K., lady, your insurance company owes my insurance company four million bucks. And you're never going to drive in this supermarket again."

"Road hog, road hog," Dorothy chanted, laughing. She pushed back. A girl at the check-out counter looked over at them as though they might be damaging the merchandise.

Whenever she was with Estelle, Dorothy became louder, more childish and happier than when she was with anyone else. Estelle drew forth other people's subversive instincts. The very first time they had met, they had ended up in Estelle's kitchen, drinking a whole bottle of sherry at two in the afternoon and telling each other their sad lives, which sounded so hopeless that they finally burst out laughing and couldn't stop for minutes. They had been friends ever since.

"Come on back for a cup of coffee?" Estelle asked.

"I'd love to, but it's got to be quick. Fred's bringing somebody back from the office."

"And you're scurrying around to fulfil all your wifely obligations. My God, I don't miss that."

"You're kidding. They're getting spaghetti and they can like it."

They were comparing recipes for meat sauce when a figure like a huge doll came trotting down one of the aisles. It was female, dressed in a sort of drum-majorette's outfit, and carried a tray with a band that went around the back of the neck. Long curls bushed out from under a species of military hat composed of metallic-painted cardbord, red glitterdust, and side rosettes. The tray was covered with tiny squares of cheese, from the centre of each one of which a tooth-pick rose straight into the air.

"Ladies, can we interest you in today's special bargain?" the girl began, and launched into a rapid sales-spiel which was almost entirely free of expressive inflection. Estelle, to stop her, reached out for one of the toothpicks and after a minute pause, during which Dorothy feared she might shove the piece of cheese into the girl's mouth, popped it into her own. But the voice went on and on, apparently unconnected with the girl's drooping gaze and scarcely moving lips. Her eyes actually looked as if she had temporarily absented herself from the Earth and were seeing from the distance of another planet. She turned her face towards one and then the other of them while her voice mentioned Swiss, American and French cheeses.

"What's it like?" Dorothy whispered.

"I'll tell you when I've finished chewing," Estelle said, pretending to have a difficult time breaking down the cheese.

The girl thrust her tray at Dorothy.

"Um, no thank you."

"There's no obligation to buy."

"Well, I'm afraid I've just bought the cheese I needed."

"This one's on special offer." It was an accusation. She offered the tray more forcefully. Dorothy took a small step backwards. The girl advanced.

"Parmesan," Dorothy said hurriedly. "It's the only kind that goes with what I'm fixing for supper. What's that like, Estelle?"

"Try it yourself," the salesgirl put in.

"Bland and boring, with an over-taste of plastic, like a processed cheese."

"This is not a processed cheese," the girl spoke up in her clearly-enunciating machine-like voice. "This cheese is made from the finest . . ."

"O.K., O.K."

Dorothy asked, "Have you sold much of it today? I mean, more than if they just put up a sign on the cheese counter?"

"You'll have to ask the publicity co-ordinator about that. I don't have the sales figures."

The girl did an about-face and tripped down the aisle again. Estelle said, "You wonder what they do to them. Not a giggle, not a reaction, not a sign of life. And so young, too."

"Processed, like the cheese. I had to do it once in the Christmas rush. You know, some people would stand there and listen to you repeat the same thing five times over."

"What were you selling?"

"Oh, some special kind of kerchief that wasn't basically any different from any other kind. All the ways you could tie it. Silly, of course. There are only two ways you can tie a scarf to make it stay on if there's a wind blowing."

"Look, there she is again."

Dorothy turned and saw a cheese-selling majorette bearing down on them.

"No, it's another one just like her."

"Good day, ladies. Can we interest you in our special cheese-of-the-day offer? This cheese, blended from the finest ingredients—"

"Oh, thanks very much, but—"

"Sorry, kid. Your friend just beat you to the draw,"

Estelle told her. "I hope you don't get commission or anything."

"Thank you anyway," Dorothy said. The girl swung around and went in search of other customers.

Estelle said, "If she's got any brains, she'll duck behind a corner and eat up half her little pieces of cheese, so they'll think she's a wonderful salesgirl."

"In a place like this, they're probably x-rayed for the toothpicks before they're allowed to go home. Have you ever seen so many tilted mirrors and hidden cameras?"

"Gives me the creeps. Really. It's a Presbyterian's dream come true—you know, God sees it all, He's watching you no matter where you are and what you're doing."

"I bet he's really out in the kitchen getting a beer out of the icebox."

"Will you look, can you believe it? There's another one."

A third salesgirl came skipping towards them. This time they tried to dodge her and for the first time noticed some sign of life in the girl, as the excitement of the hunt propelled her forward after them, chin up, eyes flashing hopefully. They were nearly at the cash registers when she caught up with them. Dorothy explained before Estelle could say something smart.

On their way to the parking lot, Dorothy said, "After all, I'm sure somebody's been drumming it into them that this is a challenge, and forcing that stuff on people is some kind of shining goal."

"Soldiers for processed cheesedom—ugh. Coming back for coffee?"

"All right, but a quick one."

Estelle drove in front. She went slowly because Dorothy was a careful driver who tended to become jumpy if rushed. Estelle, in contrast, was a natural speeder with superb reactions but a habit of looking for risks, especially if she thought she could teach another driver a lesson. It was only a matter of luck that she hadn't yet been in a serious accident or, at the very least, sued.

When they were sitting in Estelle's kitchen, Dorothy suddenly thought that she'd rather have tea, but was over-ruled by Estelle, who was proud of her coffee. Not only did she grind up the beans in a special machine, she bought the beans when they were still white, and roasted them herself.

They stopped talking while the machine was on. Estelle held her hand tight on the lid, which had a tiny nick at the side and if left alone would twist around and fly off. The sound was like a buzz saw, but didn't last long. Estelle poured the coffee into a paper filter and began to drip boiling water over it.

"Listen, Dorothy, let me tell you. You know Jeanie Cranston? Every once in a while they still have me over to meet some unattached creep. That's just an excuse. It's really to pump me about what I'm doing for the studio; glamourous snippets, names to drop with other people—you know. But I like to see Josh just to bat around old times."

"Sure, I know. Josh was nice."

" 'Don't you dare come help in the kitchen,' she says. 'You stay there and keep what's-his-name, this creep, company.' Rodge. But she'd left a plate and I forget what I wanted to ask her, but I picked up this plate and started off for the kitchen. She'd just switched on her coffee grinder—we could hear it from the table; I went through the swing door, and there was the coffee grinder screaming away empty, and there was Jeanie, spooning instant coffee into eight cups. Jesus. I mean, who's she kidding? I guess it's part of the sickness. All she ever talks about is how poor she is. They've got a yacht now. Not a big one, but, Christ, a yacht is a yacht. They charter it out when they're not using it. And the complaints about how hard it is to juggle all your taxes legally, their little place in the country, the apartment they're thinking of buying— they can rent that out, too; I should be so poor. Well. Actually, what really bothered me was Joshua."

"Fat and defeated?"

"A-1 physical shape and thinks he should be running the country. Pontificating. Right on the edge of becoming a bore. He should have come out of the closet years ago like everybody else, and then he wouldn't have to do all that compensating."

"It wouldn't have been an easy thing to take on, somebody like Jeanie. She works so hard, she really does. That's part of the trouble. She can't let up. And he's a bit incompetent. He's probably just going around with somebody twenty years younger and it's given him that little extra hint of . . ." She thought back to that time with Fred, ". . . of fraudulent righteousness," she said. "Was he praising her cooking and giving her little satisfied score-marks for doing things or saying things?"

Estelle poured the coffee and sat down at the kitchen table.

[19]

"I hadn't thought about it specially, but he was. Not for her cooking, of course. That's still TV dinner with kitchen sherry and garlic poured all over it. You really think that's a sign?"

"Oh, no, not necessarily. It just shows a general attitude. I only noticed it with Fred because he wasn't that way before. Or after. But some men are like that all the time, aren't they?"

"Josh wasn't that way before."

"Or it could be caused by something else. He might just be unhappy. Or she might be seeing somebody else."

"Oh, not her. Him, maybe."

"I know you don't think she ever knew, but maybe she did know all along. Married couples are linked to each other by such deep loyalties. You can't tell. Even when they hate each other, sometimes. I wouldn't count on either of them knowing or not knowing anything. Or how much they care."

"It could have been something else, of course. They're up to their necks in business deals at the moment. Maybe they're doing something fishy. I just had a feeling. Maybe he's done something on his own, something just over the line, so he thinks he's been a hot-shot wheeler-dealer and that's what makes him go around looking so conceited. And furtive."

"I doubt it, Estelle. His only importance comes through her. He wouldn't be able to pull a fast one by himself."

"Well, at this point, I wouldn't put it past him. He's changed a lot since you knew them."

"He must have been pontificating like crazy."

"O.K., so you think I'm exaggerating. But he was. And I was also pretty annoyed about being saddled with some dolt like that Rodge. So dim, he couldn't even size up two people like Jeanie and Josh. I don't know where they dig them up."

"Maybe they phone one of those dating clubs."

Estelle laughed. She told Dorothy a story she had heard at the studio about an extra who had been found dead in her apartment and the only clue anyone could think of was that she used to meet a lot of people through one of those places like Dateline. Dorothy said that she wouldn't be surprised; she had read a story in the papers the other day about a dating service that had turned out to be a big blackmail racket. Yes, Estelle said, and then there were the new religions and the horoscope experts and heaven knew what-all these days; it was getting so everything was as crooked as the real estate business. Dorothy said sure, but then it always was, wasn't it, and when she started to get really upset about everything, she just went out into her garden and planted something or pulled up weeds. Otherwise there was no end to it.

They talked about Estelle's two men, whom Dorothy referred to as friends or boyfriends, and Estelle gloatingly as lovers. They were named Charlie and Stan and they both wanted to marry Estelle. So far, neither one knew that the other was a real lover, only perhaps a threat. But Estelle had had enough of marriage. Her work at the studios was very well paid and full of variety and interest. She had met both Charlie and Stan through her job. They were younger than she was, nor were they the only men to be interested.

[21]

Dorothy thought Estelle was looking happy and full of vitality. The glow of health, she thought. Like a lighted candle. And what was the opposite? She remembered what Estelle had looked like before and during the divorce. It had coincided with the time of Fred's unfaithfulness. There had been many afternoons when they had sat in Estelle's kitchen and just said, "The bastards," over and over again. Dorothy had been afraid Estelle might become an alcoholic. "Don't have another drink," she would say. "Talk about it instead."

She accepted a second cup of coffee, first trying to persuade Estelle to add some water to it. Estelle was outraged. She declared that it would kill the taste.

"Then don't fill it up. Honestly, Estelle."

"Honestly yourself."

"I don't know why it doesn't have any effect on you. I love it, but two cups make me feel dizzy. And like my scalp might suddenly rise up and fly away. Then there's something over here—here, is that where the liver is?"

"Dorothy, that's where the imagination is."

They talked about Estelle's children, Sandra and Joey; and about Dorothy's plants and vegetables. Her real pride was the collection of miniature fruit trees, although she had also recently succeeded in growing apple cucumbers under glass, a feat which had delighted her at the time, and about which she was still rather pleased. They did not talk about divorce.

For a long while after her own divorce, Estelle had strongly urged Dorothy to follow suit. She had been particularly persistent, Dorothy thought, because she wanted the companionship of a similar destiny, as newly-married women want all their friends to be married, too. Or women newly become mothers, Dorothy remembered, who urge motherhood on others.

Estelle still once in a while threw out a hint about divorce, but she had really given up on Dorothy. She gave up on the day when Dorothy, worn out, had asked her to stop and explained, "I think we're too unhappy to get a divorce."

During those days there were times when Dorothy would lean her head against the wall and seem to herself to be no longer living because no longer a part of any world in which love was possible. And she had asked herself: was religion really the only thing that kept people together, wrongly believing bad things will happen after death? No, they all happen before. Especially divorce.

All at once she noticed the time and was so flustered that she almost forgot to take her package of meat out of Estelle's icebox when she left. They promised to meet on the fourteenth for the fashion show.

*   *   *   *   *

She was sweating when she got back. It was later than she had thought and she started mixing the sauce before anything else. She turned on the radio automatically between moves from stove to icebox to sink, and then sprinted to the bedroom to change her clothes and put some make-up on. As she ran back into the kitchen, snatching up the apron and tying it in back, a voice from the radio was saying: *Police again advise residents in the area to be on the lookout for this highly dangerous animal.*

Dorothy shook out and refolded her kitchen scarf to go over her head and keep her hair from picking up the garlic and onion smells. The radio played Chopin. She heard the front door closing, and Fred's voice.

From then on, things went quickly and she had to turn off the music to guard against any outside distraction. She kept her thoughts running—first this, then that, and at the same time such-and-such, and don't forget the pinch of thyme—and her hands moving. It was like some sort of test or race. Perhaps, like her, laboratory rats took a pride in solving the puzzles scientists set them. The pleasures of obsession. Still, how else was it possible to do anything in a short space of time? The trouble was, that you couldn't becalm your mind completely because if you weren't careful, you'd forget to turn off the stove.

She was into the living-room to greet Art Gruber, and out again with such speed that she might have been one of the mechanical weather-people in a child's snow-globe or a figure on a medieval clock, who zooms across a lower balcony as the face shows the hands on the hour. Back in the kitchen again, she had all the salad ingredients out, chopping up carrots and celery with her favourite sharp vegetable knife, had put some potato chips and nuts in bowls and just slid some cheese on crackers under the grill. Then she raced for the bathroom in the spare room.

She came back into the kitchen fast, to make sure that she caught the toasting cheese in time. And she was halfway across the checked linoleum floor of her nice safe kitchen, when the screen door opened and a gigantic six-foot-seven-inch frog-like creature shouldered its way into the house and stood stock-still in front of her, crouching slightly, and staring straight at her face.

She stopped before she knew she had stopped, and looked, without realizing that she was taking anything in. She was as surprised and shocked as if she had heard an explosion and seen her own shattered legs go flying across the floor. There was a space between him and the place where she was standing; it was like a gap in time. She saw how slowly everything was happening.

She felt that he was frowning at her, but he hadn't moved yet. Her mouth was slightly open—she could feel that—and waves of horripilation fled across her skin. A flash of heat or ice sped up her backbone and neck and over her scalp so that her hair really did seem to lift up. And her stomach hurt.

Then, swimming among all the startlingly released fragrances of her shock and terror, she caught the slight scent of burning, which warned her about the toast. That was the reason why she had been rushing in the first place. And without thinking, she darted forward, grabbed a potholder, turned the gas off, dumped the little pieces of toast on to the plate that had been set out for them, and slid the grill tray back into the stove.

The creature made a growling noise and she came to her senses. She took a step backwards. The growling increased. She took another step and bumped into the table. At the far end of the table lay the celery, carrots and tomatoes, the head of lettuce and her favourite sharp knife, which would cut through anything just like a razor.

She reached out her hand slowly; slowly she reached farther forward. She kept her eyes fixed on his. His eyes were huge and dark, seeming much larger than the eyes of a human being, and extremely deep. His head was quite like the head of a frog, but rounder, and the mouth was smaller and more centred in the face, like a human mouth. Only the nose was very flat, almost not there, and the forehead bulged up in two creases. The hands and feet were webbed, but not very far up, in fact only just noticeably, and as for the rest of the body, he was exactly like a man—a well-built large man—except that he was a dark spotted green-brown in colour and had no hair anywhere. And his ears were unusually small, set low down and rounded.

She stretched way out across the table, took her eyes off his for an instant and picked up the long stalk of celery next to the knife. The growling stopped. She took a step forward slowly, and held out the celery in front of her.

He too stepped forward and put his hand out. His fingers closed around the celery. She let go of her end. She stayed standing where she was and watched as he ate the stalk with all the leaves. Then she turned and picked up another one and handed it forward. This time he held on to her hand and touched it all over with both of his before he took the celery from her. The touch of his hands was warm and dry, but somehow more muscular than that of a human hand. Dorothy found it pleasant. He opened his mouth, and the lips, as though with some difficulty, shaped words.

"Thank you," he said.

Dorothy managed to answer, "You're welcome," and registered the fact that he had a bit of a foreign accent.

"I need help," he said.

She thought: you need help, my God, oh my God, you need help? You need help and so do I.

"Help me," he said. "They will kill me. I have suffered so much already."

She looked deeply into his eyes and thought: of course he has suffered, not being like other people, and now the police after him, and who knows what horrible experiments they did on him?

"All right," she told him. "But wait here first, just a minute."

She picked up the tray of toasted cheese, nuts and potato chips, and hurried into the living-room. Art gave her a perfunctory smile, but Fred didn't even look up, just muttered, "Thanks, Dotty," and went on shuffling some papers they were looking at.

She ran back through the swing door and found the frogman eating up all her salad.

"Are you hungry?" she asked. "What else do you like to eat?"

"Any vegetables," he said. He pronounced all the syllables of "vegetable", but she had met one or two ordinary Americans who said the word that way.

"Fruit?"

"Some fruit. Not too . . ." He waved his large hand and ended, "that sharp taste, not that."

"Not too acid? What about tomatoes?" She had the icebox door open and was rummaging around, putting objects in a bowl. Then she suddenly thought of the spaghetti and quickly threw some into a pot to give him before the rest of them had their dinner. While it cooked, he ate everything else, though she managed to rescue some of the salad ingredients.

She gave him spaghetti in a bowl. As she was about to spread butter on it, he growled. She got some margarine out of the icebox and used that instead. He took her wrist and leaned forward, moving his face up close to the margarine and sniffing in. Then he let go. She dropped a square of margarine into the spaghetti and swished it around until it melted. Then she sprinkled some herbs and salt on the top. He looked into the bowl, breathed in again, and seemed to be smiling. Then he picked up the bowl, held it above his face, and tipped it downwards, sucking up and chewing the spaghetti as it slipped down out of the bowl. It was a skilful performance, Dorothy thought, and rather a sensible way to eat spaghetti, but it made a lot of noise.

"I like that," he said when he had finished.

"Was it enough?"

He nodded.

"Look," she said, gesturing around her and towards the swing door into the living-room, "I've got to hide you. You understand?"

"Yes, please."

"Come with me." She handed him the bowl of vegetables he hadn't finished yet, and hurried away to the door, the hall, and into the spare room.

"You'll have to stay here. It's all right as long as you're quiet. I'll look in late tonight if I can, but probably not till early tomorrow. We'll have to plan something. There's a bed . . . um . . . and bathroom?"

He seemed to know that she was wondering if he knew what they were for and how to use them.

"Yes, just like the Institute," he said.

She showed him where all the lights were, put out some towels and sheets, and hesitated for a moment as she realized that there wasn't time to make up the bed. This too he seemed to sense, and waved it away with his hand. Then he caught both her hands in his and held them tenderly to his face. She was moved. She patted him cautiously on the back and said it was all right, and she'd see him in the morning.

In the morning, she really thought she might have dreamt everything. She made breakfast for Fred and herself, looked at the paper, took out the section with the crossword puzzle, and handed Fred the rest of the paper on the doorstep. She watched him drive off in a taxi, then she went from the kitchen into the little hallway and through to the guest room.

The frogman was still there, sitting on the corner of the bed, looking towards her. The sheets were made up on the bed. She took a step in. He stood up, huge.

"Are you all right?" she asked uncertainly.

"Yes."

"You slept?" He nodded. "Are you hungry? I'll fix you some breakfast." She led the way back to the kitchen. Halfway there, she stopped in surprise. The frame on the hall window-ledge, where she had been growing the prize apple cucumbers, was empty.

From behind her, he said, "Was it all right to eat the food? It was so long since I had food. Were you saving it?"

"No, that's all right," she said. After all, it was food, and that was what food was for. "I just hadn't expected to see it empty."

"I ate one. That was so good. I kept eating."

"I'm glad you liked them."

"Very good. Excellent. I have never had this vegetable before. Are there more?"

"No, that's why I was growing them myself. But, I can get you something like them. I'll buy in cucumbers when I go out shopping."

She cooked him some more spaghetti and tried a small amount of rice with soy sauce, which he liked very much. Once again, he ate the spaghetti by holding the plate up and letting all the contents fall slowly into his open mouth.

"My name is Dorothy," she said.

"My name is Larry."

"On the radio they said your name was Aquarius."

"That was what the professor named me when they caught me. But I couldn't pronounce it. Now I can, but now I'm used to being called Larry."

"What are you called in your own language?" Dorothy asked.

"It's too different. We don't give names."

"Isn't that confusing?"

"Everyone knows. We recognize each other."

"Do you talk?"

"That's different, too."

Dorothy waited. He looked placidly back at her.

"How?" she asked.

"More like music, but not like your music. Not jumping."

She rose from the table and switched on the radio. The foreign broadcast came on. They were playing a record of Mozart.

He said, "Is that music?"

"Yes."

"I've never heard this kind of music. They didn't have that at the Institute."

She started to turn it off, but he said, "Please, let me hear," and she left it.

"If you'll excuse me, I'll do the dishes now. Unless you'd like some more to eat."

"No, thank you."

She began to clear up the kitchen, while he watched her actions with great attention, like a child whose eyes follow its mother wherever she goes. Because he was so different, she was not bothered by him seeing her still in her bathrobe, with her hair straggling.

He asked, "Is the morning a time of festivity?"

"Just the opposite," she answered, pulling the plug out of the sink.

"Is the dress you are wearing a garment of celebration?"

"It's just my bathrobe over my nightgown. What I was wearing last night was more for a party, but not formal. It was—well, which do you like better?"

"This."

"You think it's fancier?"

"More special."

"And my hair this way?"

"Better this way."

"Is it because the dress and the hair are long now, and last night the dress was shorter and the hair was up?"

"I understand now," he said. "I like these things unrestricted. It isn't a matter of the rules of clothing. It's a question of freedom."

"To me, it's a habit. Everybody agrees that certain clothes are worn for certain activities. Once the habit is accepted, it means something. And then, to break it means something too."

"For me, clothes aren't necessary. I don't see a meaning."

"For protection from the weather, for warmth and to keep the skin from too much sun, or from being cut and scratched."

"My skin is strong," he said. He lifted her hand from where she had been wiping the tabletop and placed the hand on his arm. He rubbed it from high up near his shoulder down to his wrist. She was shocked and pleased. Long after her hand was away from him, it seemed to remember the feel of his arm: warm, smooth and muscled.

"Yes," she said. "If you'll excuse me now, I generally clean up in the mornings, and then afterwards we can sit down and decide what we're going to do about you."

"I can clean, too?"

"Well," she laughed, "come keep me company, that's all."

"You could show me what to do. You see, I'm not used to this. It's so different. Before, I was only being studied. There was nothing. Now there's everything. I could do things. Couldn't I? You wouldn't prevent me?"

"Of course not. The only thing you'd better not do is go outdoors in the daytime. It would probably be all right at night."

She rinsed the cloth, hung it up by the sink, and went through the doorway and hall, into the guest room. He followed her, closing the door and shutting out the sound of the Mozart. She turned to ask him if he still wanted the radio on, and saw by the light—bright although blocked by the curtains—that when he had asked if she would prevent him from doing what he wanted to do, he might have meant something quite specific. That was another reason, which she had been too prim to mention, for wearing clothes.

He stepped forward, took off her bathrobe, letting it fall on top of the bed, and started to take off her nightgown from top to bottom, but quickly realized that it must be made to work the other way. He picked up the skirt from around her knees and lifted it over her head. He put his hand on her shoulder and pushed her gently down on the bed. He sat beside her. He said, looking at her, "I've never seen. Men, but not someone like you."

"A woman," she whispered, her throat beginning to close up.

He asked, "Are you frightened?"

"Of course."

"I'm not. I feel good. But it's very strange."

A lot more than strange, she thought. And then: no,

it's just the same. They rolled backwards together on the bed.

"Wait. Not like that," she said.

"Show me."

"I'm a bit embarrassed."

"What does that mean?"

She didn't really know. What the hell could it mean in such an encounter?

Later in the day, when they were lying side by side, she asked, "Are you young, or are you old, or are you in between?"

"I'm between young and in-between. And you?"

"So am I, but I'm afraid I'm nearer to in-between now than to young. In the middle."

"Is this time worse for you than it was before?"

"Not now. Now it's better."

They made love on the living-room floor and on the dining-room sofa and sitting in the kitchen chairs, and upstairs in the bathtub. And they talked. Most of their talk consisted of asking and answering questions. She asked him, "Where do you come from? Does everyone make love so many times in one day?"

"Is it too much?"

"No. It's just the right amount for me. It's perfect. People here are all different about it: some people like a lot, some only like a little, some change according to who they're with or what age they are or whether they're in a good mood, or even if the weather changes."

He told her about the two men, Kelsoe and Wachter, who had mistreated him. They had taught him human speech, using an electronic gadget which gave him a shock every time he got something wrong. The teaching scheme was run by a Dr Forest, who was severe but emotionally detached. When he went away, Kelsoe and Wachter used the electric prod and other devices—the chair with the straps and the fitted eyeglasses—to tease and torture. They had also, he later told her, taken advantage of their positions of power in order to force his participation in various forms of sexual abuse, some of which she hadn't known of before. That first hesitant approach down in the guest room must have been because of what they had done to him at the Institute. She tried to explain. He said it didn't matter—he could tell that this was different. She felt incapable of making him understand how such a thing could have happened, and why the same thing done from different motives could be either good or bad, and what those ideas meant. She would have liked to say: it's the lack of love. But that too was hard to talk about. In highschool she had been asked to write essays like that: Love, Beauty, Time. Time had been the most interesting. She had written fifteen pages on that before the bell rang. But, of course, you could see Time. It was easier to write about something you could see, or of which you could see the effects.

He took showers often, several throughout the day. He liked watching television, and most of all he liked music. As for his diet, she was soon to find it no more out of the ordinary than that of the average man on a health-food kick.

That first day, she brought in her tape measure before going out to do her afternoon shopping. She measured his feet and wrote down the numbers on a piece of paper.

"I know your skin is strong, but you'll have to get some exercise, and if you go walking around here late at night, there's always a chance of picking up a nail or some broken glass. And the sidewalks can be hard."

"It's true. Last night when I came into the kitchen, my feet were hurting very much."

"I'll try to find you some sandals."

"Thank you," he said. He was always scrupulously polite. Now that she knew of the brutal methods that had been used to ram home the Institute's policy on polite manners, she found these little touches of good breeding in his speech as poignant as if they had been scars on his body.

When she left the house, she told him about the phone and the doorbell, gave him a key to his room, and warned him to keep the volume down if he wanted to listen to the radio or watch television.

She drove off to do her shopping like a young girl setting out on her first job. Not even the sarcastic attitude of the man in the shoeshop could entirely spoil the outing.

"What's this for, lady, the abominable snowman? Are you kidding?"

"For my brother-in-law," she answered calmly. "He has to get his shoes hand-made. And now his luggage was stolen, he's in a fix. He told us how it used to be when he was in school—how people in the shoeshops would laugh at him and make jokes. I never believed it before. I couldn't imagine people would laugh at a natural physical condition."

"All right, all right, you're breaking my heart."

Heart? She could picture the man with an electric prod in his hand. He called down the stairs to the storeroom. A voice answered from below, and a few moments later a boy with long greyish hair handed up a shoebox.

"Just as long as the measurements are right."

"This is the right size." She thought he would leave it at that, but he couldn't resist. "Any bigger than that," he added, "and he'll have to wear the boxes."

Even without the extra money for the sandals, she spent more than she had intended to. She bought extra vegetables, noodles, more rice, an extravagant pack of wild rice, and avocados, which she saw just as she was ready to head for the cash registers.

Her happiness returned, like a glow, as though she had swallowed something warm which was continuing to radiate waves of the warmth. It was a secret thing of her very own, yet she also wanted to talk about it to someone. This was the way she had felt the last time she had been pregnant. Could she say something to Estelle? If Estelle didn't understand, if she ever dropped a hint to anyone, the police would be at the door with pistols and truncheons, or the doctors with injections of drugs, which might be even worse. They would say it was for the good of society, perhaps even for Larry's own good. And there was the evidence of the two killings to back up any such claims. On the way to the shoeshop she had turned on the radio and heard the news bulletin, which told how one of the men, the one named Kelsoe, had had his head literally torn from his body, while the other one had been "ripped in two and gutted".

It was better not to tell anyone, though she would have to plan out what they would do if he were seen by accident.

She was thinking of outsiders. Fred wouldn't notice anything because he never came near those rooms. In fact, he seldom came into the kitchen. He even preferred to have breakfast at the dining-room table. Years ago, they had been in the kitchen all the time, and Scotty too. That was a long while back now.

She left the highway, drove straight on, turned off into the street that ran by the plant nurseries, passed the fancy villas with their big gardens, and went around the corner. There, up in the sky, she noticed for the first time a gigantic mounded cloud, as large and elaborately moulded as a baroque opera house and lit from below and at the sides by pink and creamy hues. It sailed beyond her, improbable and romantic, following in the blue sky the course she was taking down below. It seemed to her that it must be a good omen.

*   *   *   *   *

*A*t supper Fred was quiet, as usual. He had papers to see to, he said. And she, also as usual, retired to the kitchen.

She prepared a massive salad for Larry, took it through into the hall, and gave the prearranged knock on the door.

She sat with him for a few minutes while he ate, but soon decided that it would be better if she stayed in the kitchen. The phone might ring, or Fred might call through to her about something and, not hearing an answer, come on in and find them both.

"I'll be back later, when it's dark, and we'll take a walk." She looked at his feet in the sandals. "Are they comfortable?"

"All right. They're like clothes." He turned from the television set, the old black-and-white one, which he was watching with the sound turned off. He picked a slice of avocado out of the salad, lowered it into his mouth and moved his lips. He said, "This is the best vegetable I have had so far. It's what I like most."

"Good. I'm glad."

"May I have it for breakfast, please?"

"Yes, of course."

She washed dishes and wondered how much the extra food was going to put on their weekly expenses. It probably wouldn't make any difference to Fred—prices were going up so fast anyway. At least they were in a part of the world where avocados were not exorbitantly expensive. Lucky he didn't like lobster or shrimps.

The phone rang. As she picked up the receiver, she remembered that she had meant to phone her sister-in-law about their vacation.

"Dorothy?" It was Estelle.

"Oh, hi Stelle. I was going to call you. I haven't gotten around to anything today."

Estelle reminded her about the fashion show and asked if she and Fred would like to come to a party on the following Saturday. Dorothy pushed the swing door, went through the dining-room, and put her head around the corner. Fred was sitting at the desk, his cheek propped against his fist, his weight on his left elbow. It didn't look as though he could be working very hard. She asked him about Saturday. He answered, "No", automatically, without even turning his head.

"You sure? It might be fun."

"Not for me. You go if you like."

"Well, I might. I'd rather go with you." He said nothing and didn't move. She went back to the kitchen.

"Estelle? Fred says no."

"Why not?"

"Oh, I don't know why not. He isn't doing anything but just sitting. But he says no."

"You come."

"I might. Let me wait a few days. I'll tell you when I see you for the fashion show."

"O.K. See you then."

It was true, Dorothy thought: he wasn't really working. She put the receiver back, got Larry's salad bowl from him, and told him to be ready. They would take the car. Fred never minded where she went any more, or when. At first, after Scotty and the baby, when she had begun the compulsive restless walks, he had been worried about her. He had fussed. She was unprotected, he said. Anything could happen, even in the suburbs, even in a nice one like theirs. People weren't like eggs in boxes—they didn't have to stay in their own neighbourhood. They could move around. Yes, she had said, and now she wanted to do some moving around herself. She ought to get a dog at least, he had told her, for protection. All right, she had said, all right. She had bought a dog; a little, upright, friendly dog called

a Jack Russell terrier. She named him Bingo and took
him home. Fred exploded. "Call that a dog?" he had
shouted. "It's smaller than a loaf of bread." "He's very
quick," she had explained, "and his attention never
leaves you. He's—" "Oh, Jesus Christ, Dot. You
would go get some useless toy dog like that. Fat lot of
good that would be if you turn the corner and bump
into a gang of roughs who'd beat you up and rape
you." "With my luck," she had screamed, "they'd tie
me to the railings and rape the dog instead." He had
hit her, in order, he had explained later, to calm her
down, and she had begun to sob and asked why he
had wanted the twin beds and why they never slept
together any more, even just to be together. He had
said it made him feel guilty, because he just couldn't,
because nothing was right any longer, but it would
blow over if only they would let things alone. It might
take time, but they'd get back to normal eventually,
and in the meantime, if she just wouldn't put any pres-
sure on him. Sure, she had said, it would work out.

She had taken Bingo on walks. They had walked
everywhere. She had never seen such a lively little
animal. It was fun to be with him, he was so delighted
by being alive. He retained his playfulness even after
leaving the puppy stage. He was just becoming a full-
grown dog when one day she looked up from planting
some bulbs in the garden and didn't see him. He didn't
come back all day. He didn't come back because he
had been hit by a car. Fred had found her crying in
the living-room when he came home. Everything near
her died, she had said. Everything; it was a wonder
the grass on the front lawn didn't turn around and

sink back into the earth. She cried for days, weeks. And Fred began to explain less and even to talk less. No matter how much you loved someone, there was a limit to the amount of crying you could stand hearing.

From that time onwards, he hadn't tried to stop her going out of the house alone at night, or even asked where she was going or when she would be coming back.

She put her head around the corner again and told him she thought she'd mail some letters and take the car for a drive. He just said, "O.K." He was sitting in the same position he had been in before.

She went in to Larry, took him by the hand, led him through the hall and the kitchen, and through the door they hardly ever used, the one that connected directly to the inside of the garage. She opened the car door and stowed him in the back. He was too large to have fitted comfortably with his head down on the front seat. She put her straw bag on the seat beside her.

The evening was clear and a light breeze moved here and there. It wasn't quite dark yet. She drove down the straight, neat streets in the soft, lingering twilight. All the houses looked lovely in this light, with some lamps on but not many curtains drawn. There had been a time when she could not bear seeing lighted houses in the evening hour, because they had made her think how many of those houses represented a family, and how many of them contained children.

"I wish you could sit up and look, but it's still too light. Somebody might see you from one of the windows. It won't be long now. I'll tell you when."

"I can smell the gardens," he said.

She too could smell the flowers, giving out their fragrance as the light went, and the grass, which reminded her of her own childhood in school during the month of May and the early days of June, when all the windows were open and the men were out cutting the grass on the playing fields.

"I love it," she said. "But a friend of mine from school used to get hay fever. She couldn't get near any grass or trees or plants without coughing and sneezing —every year. I suppose by now she must be taking pills or getting injections for it."

"For me, it's like food."

"Me too, especially flowers." She wondered if he would like perfume. Fred hated it. He couldn't even stand any scented soap other than Palmolive.

She drove until they reached a stretch containing relatively few houses. The air was darker now, the leaves of the trees almost black by the sides of the road and hanging down from above.

"I think it's all right now, Larry. But be ready to duck down if I tell you." She saw his face come up in the driving mirror. He looked ahead, and to either side. After a while, he said, "If I had a hat, do you think I would be noticed at night?"

"It would need more than a hat. I think with make-up and sunglasses you might just get away with it. If you drove fast."

"Could you teach me to make the car go?"

"Oh, yes. That part would be easy."

She headed for the beach. On the highways he stayed crouched down in the seat again, until they emerged into a quiet, slightly run-down neighbourhood full of old clapboard houses and tattered palm trees. Here the buildings were closer to the sidewalks and there were few flowers. In many of the front yards there was just a square of sandy ground instead of grass. Faintly from the background, like the swish of traffic on a main road, Dorothy heard the sea. From the back seat Larry gave forth a soft moan of pleasure or pain. He had heard it, too.

"I brought some towels. We could go swimming, if you like."

"Yes, please."

She turned off, along a sandy road. No one was around. She branched off again on to a narrow, bumpy path and stopped the car. The sea was loud and near.

He climbed over the back seat and sat next to her. He put his arm around her. She leaned her head on his shoulder. They sat still, listening.

She thought: all during my teens, when I kept wishing so hard for this—to be out in a car on the beach with a boy—and it never happened. But now it's happened.

He said, "You hear?"

"Yes, I've always loved the sound of the sea. I think everybody does."

"For me, it's the sound of where I live. That's hard to explain. It's always there, like your heartbeats. Always, for our whole lives, we have music. We have wonderful music. The sea speaks to us. And it's our home that speaks. Can you understand?"

"You must be lonely."

"More than anything. More than hunger. Even hunger sometimes goes away, but this doesn't."

She stroked his face with her hand. She tried to imagine what his world could be like. Perhaps it was like a child floating in its mother's womb and hearing her voice all around him.

She asked, "What was it like?"

"So many things are different. Colour is different. Everything that you see tells you something. At the Institute, they told me there are some people who are colour-blind. When you show them, they don't believe it at first. They can't believe they suffer from this thing, because they have never known any other way. That's how difficult it would be to explain the difference in the way my world looks."

"And the sound."

"And the way it feels. When you move, the place you live in moves too."

"Your eyes are specially developed for seeing underwater, aren't they? I mean, I'm not sure that I'd see what you see, even if I could go down there in a diving suit."

"Yes, they were very interested in my eyes."

"When you escaped, did the light hurt your eyes?"

"Yes."

"Then the idea about sunglasses was a good one after all. I'll have to get you a pair, just in case."

"I took a hat to begin with. It cut off some of the light."

An ordinary pair of dark glasses wouldn't work, of course. His head was much too big. She'd have to take off the earpieces and widen the central frame somehow, and then put everything back together. And would the two lenses be far enough apart, anyway? There was also the problem of where to rest the nose-bridge, since the space between his eyes was flat and his eyes swelled outwards; it would hurt to have the glass lenses bumping right up against his eyes.

"If you swam out into the sea now, could you get back to your home?"

"No," he said sadly. "They showed me on a map where it was that they captured me, and it's far away."

"Could you show me on a map?"

"Yes. It's called the Gulf of Mexico."

"I see what you mean. You'd have to swim all the way down the coast and get through the Panama Canal."

"You know, it's wonderful to see another world. It's entirely unlike anything that has ever come to your thoughts. And everything in it fits. You couldn't have dreamed it up yourself, but somehow it all seems to work, and each tiny part is related. Everything except me. If I had known I was only going to stay a short while, this would have been the most exciting thing I could imagine—a marvel in my life. But to know that it's for ever, that I'll always be here where I'm not able to belong, and that I'll never be able to get back home, never . . ."

He bowed his head. She embraced him.

"I don't know how I could bear to give you up now," she told him. "Now that you've come, everything's all right." She talked about her marriage and about her children. "But I understand. If I could manage to get you to the coastline on the nearest point to your home, could you swim from there?"

"Yes," he said, raising his head.

"Then we can get you back. We'd have to work it so that you swim down the shore while I drive the car across the Mexican border, and then once I was over, I'd pick you up."

They talked about the idea. The actual plan seemed simple enough. It was only the timing that might be difficult. Fred's vacation was coming up and there was also the question of his sister, Suzanne, whom he didn't much care for himself, but had always pushed on to Dorothy whenever Suzanne had felt the need to see him again. Suzanne was supposed to be visiting them sometime during the next two months.

There had been a few years when they had taken separate vacations, or when he had gone on his and she had stayed at home. Sometimes she went to see her parents, who were old now and occasionally irritating to be with; first one of them more than the other, then the order reversed, often nowadays both equally peevish. Could she just take the car and say she was off for a break?

Larry removed his sandals and stepped out of the car. She followed, bringing the keys and the basket holding the towels.

At first they swam together. She was amazed at the difference in his mood. It was like being in the water with a beachball, but also a powerful animal or machine. The way he looked had not convinced her of his difference, but this did: the way he moved in the water, which was his element. He came rocketing up from the deep water and picked her up in his arms, driving across the waves with her. They seemed to be going as fast as a motorboat.

After a while, Dorothy said that she wanted to get out and get dry. Larry asked her to wait while he explored.

"Be careful," she told him. "The coast around here has a narrow shelf under the water and then it drops right down deep. There's no gradual sloping."

She walked up the beach, dried herself off, and put on her clothes. Then she sat down and waited, and tried to think out a plan. For so many years there had been nothing. She had taken jobs to keep herself busy, but that was all they were. She had had no interests, no marriage to speak of, no children. Now, at last, she had something.

What they ought to do was tell the world. There was only one word for what those terrible people at the Institute had done to him: torture. They could take it to the newspapers. Especially the part about those two men forcing him to join them in their sex games. *I Killed Defending My Manhood.* You could take it to the Supreme Court. You could plead disorientation. It would cause a sensation. It would be a test case. They'd have to define the nature of the term *human being.* If Larry wasn't human, he couldn't commit murder, only kill like an animal and not be punished for it. On the other hand, if he were to be considered human, he had killed in a self-protective anger brought on by pain caused through torture by two sadists, who had taken away his human rights and wrongfully imprisoned him in the first place just because he was of a different race. She could imagine the headlines: *These cruel and barbaric practices are not consistent with the teachings of our religion, says frogman. Is this the spirit of American Democracy, we ask?*

But he had told her that all he wanted to do was go back home. He wouldn't want to go to the newspapers. He was right, of course. It wasn't just the crowds and the bright lights and the fast-talking media men and the people who ran forward to spit at you. It was also possible—as the announcer had said on the radio—that a simple disease, even a cold, could kill a creature who had never developed a resistance to it. Even worse, perhaps he might already be carrying a germ which would not declare itself to be fatal until after he returned home, so innocently bringing with him the means of destroying his whole people. Better not think about that.

She ought to try to get him away soon, but she couldn't leave just like that. She'd have to have some excuse. She'd have to wait till the vacation.

He was gone a long time, it seemed. The warm wind had blown the skies clear so that she could see the stars. She wondered what he was doing, how far out he had swum, how deep. She thought of him swimming among the wonderful colours, in surroundings which would be different from his home, but familiar —as though a man from Connecticut had been kidnapped to a foreign planet and then set down again in Norway or Japan; it wouldn't be home, yet it would be recognizable.

But down there it would be dark now, and not the

lovely lighted aquarium she imagined it to be during
the daylight hours, eddying with schools of tiny, delicate animals floating and dancing slowly to their own
serene currents and creating the look of a living paint-
ing. That was wrong, in any case. The ocean was
different from an aquarium, which was an artificial
environment. The ocean was a world. And a world is
not art. Dorothy thought about the living things that
moved in that world: large, ruthless and hungry. Like
us up here.

She was just beginning to convince herself that down
at the bottom of the sea he was hurt or dying, when
she saw his shape moving up out of the water. In that
light and at a distance, he looked exactly like the statues
of gods, except that his head was slightly larger and
rounder than it should be. And he walked with a
rounded, swimming motion from hip to knee, holding
his large, powerful shoulders and arms easily.

She handed him a towel and he dried himself off.

"Shall I start teaching you how to drive, or would
you rather leave it for tomorrow? It's a little late now.
I didn't know you'd be so long."

"Tomorrow," he said.

"Are you cold?"

"No."

He climbed into the back seat again. Dorothy started
the car. "This would be a good place to learn," she
said. "There doesn't seem to be anyone around and
that path over there runs for a long way, just a
straight stretch."

She told him about her plan. Could he wait that
long? He said yes. She asked him what it had been

like in the water. He answered that it was not like his home; he had felt almost as foreign there as above the surface.

"But down there, I know how to defend myself. Down there no one attacks you for thinking. They attack if you hurt them or invade their home, or if they want to eat you."

"And if you're different. They do that here, too."

"But in the sea, it's not just because you're different."

"I thought everywhere everyone had to fit in, or other people began to feel worried and threatened. And then if there are more of them than of you, they jump on you."

"That happens here?"

"More or less. It's true that what happens first is they let you know how they think, and then you've got to make them believe you think that. Something else happened. You're sad."

"Yes. Something is going on."

"The Institute does a lot of underwater research around here. You mean that?"

"No. I don't know. It didn't feel right."

"It isn't where you come from."

"Do you suppose I've changed? Maybe they did something to me in the experiments, which I didn't know about at the time, to make it so I can never go back and be at peace. They injected me a lot, you know, so I fell asleep."

Dorothy stopped the car at the side of the road, leaned over into the back seat and put her arms around his neck. She kissed him and patted him on the back.

"Don't worry. It'll work out somehow." She was about to turn back to the wheel, when he said, "Could we walk?"

They were not very far from the house, but in a richer neighbourhood, in a street of large houses standing in gardens, with trees lining the sidewalks. She got out, telling him to be careful closing the door.

They walked hand in hand. At one point Larry stood still, breathing deeply. He said that there was a flower he could smell. He took off his sandals and prowled across a large grass lawn to a flowerbed. Dorothy followed, hoping that the owners of the houses would keep any dogs inside rather than outside. When she caught up with him, he had his face in some white flowers which she identified as the blossoms of a tobacco plant. They walked through the gardens for twenty minutes or so before deciding to go home.

During the next few days, they settled down into a routine. At night they drove out. They swam, never for such a long time as that first night, and then she gave him driving lessons. He was very quick to learn. She bought him a hat which she enlarged, sunglasses, which she altered specially for him, and some make-up, with which they experimented until he said that he thought he'd like different colours. Dorothy had made him up in a beige colour. But when he got hold of the box himself, he made himself up in three different shades: yellow-brown, red-brown and a dark brown.

"The hands," Dorothy said.

"Gloves. Which one do you think is best?"

"The Indian one looks the best, but it's too unusual. I think maybe the Chinese one."

"I thought it was more Japanese. You don't like the black one?"

"It doesn't look natural. I don't know why."

"They don't any of them look natural, but under those lights on the highway nobody looks natural."

"Still, people would notice a man with a green head. I guess I should get you a wig."

"Good. I think I'll try a different colour every night."

When Dorothy went out shopping, Larry generally listened to music or watched television. It was from a crime-story serial on television that he got the idea of starting a car without any keys by pulling the leads out and sparking them off. The first Dorothy knew of it was when she went to his room to tell him she would be ready in ten minutes, and found that he had gone.

All the rest of that evening she waited up in the kitchen. He hadn't taken the car, but his hat was missing, and the glasses, sandals, suit, socks and gloves. She was so worried that when he finally came back she was ready to hit him out of relief and fury.

"Where have you been?" she hissed, bundling him through the hall and into his room. "Walking around town as free as you please. I've told you, you've got to be careful."

"I was driving."

"The car was in all night. I checked."

"I took a different car. Just in case I was caught and they traced me back to you. You might get into trouble, you know, for protecting a dangerous criminal. Knowledge after the event—that's it, isn't it?"

She made him sit down on the bed. He told her where he had gone and what he had seen. After he'd convinced her that no one had recognized him or followed him, he admitted that he had gotten out of the car and walked. He had walked through crowds, where many of the men were drunk and no one would want to pick a fight with someone of his size in any case. "And I've figured out the make-up. The secret is to wear a colour that's different from most of the people who live in the area."

"I still don't understand how you started the car."

"I'll show you tomorrow. It was easy, but I was a little nervous at first. You know I don't like electricity."

"Would you rather go out alone at night?" Dorothy asked. "I mean, I'd worry, but you see so much of me during the day—would it help to make you feel you have some independence?"

Larry removed his gloves and took her hand in his. "You understand," he said.

"What I'd really like would be if we could be free to walk around anywhere, go out for a meal together in a restaurant, and so on."

"I thought people were supposed to enjoy what they call 'a secret vice'," he said, and made her laugh so hard that she nearly ripped the wig which she had started to put back in its box. She had sewn and cut his wig herself, making it from two she had bought, since a single one would not have been big enough.

"And am I your secret vice?" she asked.

"No, my secret vice is avocados."

Dorothy laughed even harder. She had to bury her face in the bedclothes to hide the noise.

* * * * *

*T*wo days after Larry began his independent nightly drives, Dorothy went to see Estelle in the afternoon.

"You look different," Estelle said. "You've gotten Suzanne off your back."

Dorothy said no, Suzanne had given them four different sets of detailed instructions concerning her plans for the coming three months. Dorothy sat down. "And I bet there'll be a new set in the mail soon. She used to call up, till I pretended the phone was out of order."

She had great difficulty in controlling herself. Estelle would understand; but, she would also tell. She wouldn't be able to resist it. And would that be strange, when Dorothy herself was having so much trouble trying to keep herself from speaking? Better not even think about it. The thought was compelling. It was like people who looked down from a height.

"Coffee," Estelle asked, already pouring it out. Sandra and Joey wandered into the kitchen separately, stared glumly, had to be told to say hello, opened the icebox for food, ate standing up and shuffled out again. When they were beyond the door and out of earshot, Estelle muttered, "They sometimes seem hardly human. I keep telling myself it's a phase. They're so crass and surly and just godawful. All they say is Yaah and Naah. At first I thought they were drugged."

"Maybe they are."

"No, no, that I'm sure of."

"They've got hormones shooting through their systems a mile a minute—those are drugs. I see what you mean, though. When I was that age, I was all dimity and feminine and dreamy, reading poetry and so on."

"Were you? I was out in a back seat with Jimmy McGraw from the other side of the tracks. Best nights of my life. After the divorce, I thought of tracking all those people down, and then I thought what's the use. The whole point about it was that it was then, not now."

"That figures."

"What I mean is . . . you're right, it doesn't make sense. You know what I mean."

"It may be something to do with fitting in with the others, too."

"Like those Irish children. It's—no, I threw it out. It was an article in a magazine: they did a sociological survey on children from several different families where the parents wanted at least one child to go into the church. And what they found was that these children were chosen quite early. You could see they were nice-looking and obedient and neat, whereas their sisters and brothers became plain and bad-tempered and sloppy-looking. What was interesting about the study was that after the children had been chosen and the time of danger had passed, the other children suddenly blossomed and stopped being plain and slovenly. I mean, they also seemed to change physically."

"A subconscious defence. And the other ones were conforming to expectation. They'd stay that way, too."

"But Jesus, Dorothy, I'm not trying to put my kids into the church."

"Don't be silly. They're like any other teenagers. As a matter of fact, you're lucky they're not being brainwashed by one of those freak cults, told to break with their family and so forth. After that Jones business, anything is possible. And the teens are the dangerous age for religion. I felt that way myself."

"You're kidding," Estelle said. "You? I thought you were my one reasonable friend."

"Oh, you know. All those feelings of holiness and beauty and love. What else tries to explain them? Then you look around at most of the men and women you see, and you think that's certainly not enough, that's just routine. Let's say it was romance. Your instinct for romance is very powerful in your teens."

"Romance, right. That's different. Romance and tragedy. Except, now I'm older, what I really go for is comedy. Even the international situation. My God, what a circus."

"Which reminds me," Dorothy said, "how are Charlie and Stan? They know about each other yet?"

"Oh-ho. Sixty-four-dollar question. I think Charlie knows that there's someone, but doesn't know who it could be. He actually thought there was someone when there wasn't yet."

"And Stan?"

"Him, he's so conceited it would never cross his mind."

"Is he so good-looking?"

"Didn't I show you the picture?"

"I didn't think it was so special."

"He's better in the flesh, as they say."

"But Charlie's better in bed?"

"You're not supposed to be able to guess these things so easily. Let's talk about you. Let's talk about your new lover."

"Oh, come on. Me? What you could talk about that would help me, would be how I can get Suzanne off my neck."

"Is she coming with her kids, or alone? Or with what's-his-name?"

"Bruce. Not this time. Just Suzanne all by herself. I almost prefer it when they all come. They're fighting with each other so hard, you don't even have to say much, just sit there and listen. And I get a kick out of seeing Fred start to get hysterical but trying to contain himself. He doesn't like them either, even Suzanne. Why he won't admit it, why he keeps shoving her on to me . . . to be fair, I thought Robin wasn't so bad last time. She's a funny-looking girl, though."

"With the Brillo-pad head, like her mother?"

"Just the opposite. You know the Charles Addams cartoon of the thin wife with the long, stringy hair? Robin's like that, but instead of wearing a long dress that tapers down to where she disappears into the rug, she's usually wearing pants and cowboy boots. She says she wants to be a choreographer. She says she has an idea for a whole series of ballets based on the chemical combinations of molecules in action, or something like that. She drew me a picture. It looked great. Really. But she won't be coming. Just Suzanne."

"The only way really to get rid of her is to leave the house yourself when she arrives. You know, pack everything, and the minute you see her marching up the path, you just march right out the door with your suitcases."

"I thought of that," Dorothy said, and sighed.

"Fred could take her off your hands if he'd just make an effort."

"Well, I see what he means. He can't do much if he's working all day."

"Working. That's what they all say."

"Well, it's true."

"It's not work like real work, like us."

"Estelle, you're terrific. We're so exploited, we're spending our afternoons sitting around drinking coffee."

"Another cup," Estelle said. She managed, as usual, to over-ride Dorothy's protests.

They talked about the studio. Dorothy said that in a few months, she might ask Estelle to set up another job for her. Not now, but in five months' time or so. By that time, Larry would have gone back to his home again, and she would not dare to stay in the house, mooning around the back rooms, thinking about how everybody always left or died. Years before, when she thought she was just about to sink like a stone, it had been the jobs which had brought her back to life again. There had even been other people she had met through the work, who might also have helped, but she hadn't seen that at the time. And meanwhile, she and Fred had lost a lot of friends and stopped going out much.

As Dorothy started to leave, Estelle said, "I'll pick you up for the show. The place will probably be packed and we'll have to fight for a parking space."

They agreed on the time and Dorothy thanked Estelle again for the Saturday invitation, but said that since Fred wasn't coming, she'd ask for a raincheck too. She started off in the direction of home, then changed her mind and stopped to buy some avocados.

When she got home, Fred was there before her. He said, "I may have to go out again. I've got a deal on."

"With Art?"

"That's right," he said, so quickly that she knew it wasn't true.

"Some time I want to talk about Suzanne and what we're going to do about the vacation."

"O.K., O.K., only not now."

"All right. Just remember that I don't want her here until after we get back."

"All right, all right."

"You aren't listening."

"After we get back. Mr Mendoza left a note about the garden. Where were you? You're out driving in the car all the time. A hundred bucks a minute if the price of gas goes up any more."

Dorothy picked up a crumpled paper from the desk. She looked at it, turned it over, and said, "Could you make out what this means? All I can read is, 'Dear Mess Jade'. Usually his writing is so neat. He must have been in a hurry."

"Well?"

"That's all. Unless this word is supposed to mean Saturday."

"Where were you this afternoon?"

"What? Oh, at Estelle's," Dorothy answered, still peering at the letter. "Honestly, can't you help?" She handed the paper to him. He took it, but did not look at it. He looked at her instead.

"What?" she said.

"I called Estelle. She said you weren't there."

"Of course I wasn't there. I'd just left."

"It took you a long time to get home."

"I went shopping. What is this? You can call Estelle and ask her when I arrived and when I left."

"What did you get when you were shopping?"

"Avocados," Dorothy said. She turned from him, strode to the kitchen, picked up the brown-paper bag and brought it to him.

"Oh, I believe you," he said. She unrolled the top of the bag so that he could see what was inside. All at once the tight, ironic, play-acting expression went out of his face. He said, "The whole bagful? You bought a whole bag of avocados? Jesus, there must be twenty of them in there. What on earth for? We'll never get through them. They'll go bad."

"No, they won't. I'll eat them."

"Dorothy, that's crazy."

Dorothy closed the top of the bag. Her voice rose. "It isn't crazy," she insisted. "It's a special avocado diet. You lose several pounds all at once and just keep going."

"They're fattening as hell."

"Not if you don't put anything on them. And it's all a question of balance, anyway. Once you get settled in the diet, the trace elements start burning up all your fat, or something like that."

"You could always buy gold-dust instead. In the first place, you don't need to go on a diet, and in the second place, if you did, you could go on one by just eating less than normal. A whole bag—honestly, Dot, it's crazy. It looks like the treasure of the Aztecs. A whole bag."

"Never mind. You won't have to eat any if you don't want to."

The phone rang. There was a tiny, electric moment between them and then Fred grabbed for the phone.

"Yes," he said, "yes. No. About half an hour. O.K."

Dorothy wondered what would have happened if she had answered, instead. An even shorter conversation: wrong number.

"What time are you coming back?" she asked.

"Before midnight, I hope."

"I'll want the car," she said. "Do you mind?"

"Couldn't you just—"

"No, I need to be able to get out. Didn't the garage offer you anything?"

"It wasn't supposed to take this long."

"Oh, Fred, it always takes this long. Everything on that museum piece has to be fixed by a fanatic. They have to scour the countryside for experts and then they have to make all the missing parts from scratch."

He picked up the telephone receiver again and called a cab.

Dorothy held up Mr Mendoza's note in front of him.

"I don't know," he said. "One of the words is 'tomatoes'."

"That's 'tomorrow'."

"It's about the only one I can understand."

The taxi arrived, driven by someone who looked like an eleven-year-old girl with a beard. He had on a big leather jacket and walked up to the door very slowly, not like most of the taxicab hustlers in town. Fred answered the bell and went back down the path with the boy. He turned around to wave at Dorothy, who raised her hand in return. He hadn't done that for years.

She went back to the kitchen, where she forgot what she had intended to do next, and sat down in a chair by the kitchen table. He was asking her all those questions too, almost as if he suspected her. It might be because he himself felt guilty, or maybe she did unconsciously give out some signal that she was again a desired woman.

She made a large salad, which she tossed in the Hawaiian wooden bowl. All over the top she laid long slices of avocado. Her father's family had called them "alligator pears", but she hadn't told Larry. She thought he might be hurt somehow. The ones she had bought were the smooth, thin-skinned type, though she had seen others that really did look like the hide of an alligator: dark green and knobbly outside, with thicker skins. Inside, the edible part was exactly the same.

She took another quick look at Mr Mendoza's note. It must mean tomatoes after all. She had forgotten that this was his day, but he would be back the next week.

She carried salad and plates into Larry's room. He was listening to her foreign broadcast of classical music, but turned it off as she came in sideways with the tray.

Over their meal he said, "I was watching TV before he came in."

"Something nice?"

"An old movie called *Marie Antoinette*."

"They must have put it on because of the fashion show. Some of the costumes from the film are going to be there. That's where I'm going with Estelle on Thursday."

"That would be interesting."

"I wish you could come too."

"That would be even more interesting. As a matter of fact, I've also been looking at the news and current affairs, and you can't imagine what they've been saying about me. And in how many states I've been seen. The monster this, the monster that. Why should people make up such things? No one has seen me, and yet they say it and they even appear to believe it. Why?"

"That's hard to explain. Sometimes it's just to feel important. Sometimes they see something unclear and very quickly, and don't know what it is; a shadow behind a tree, or something, but they exaggerate."

"No, they invent. I'm asking because I want to know whether this is a basic human characteristic."

"I don't know about basic. It's pretty common, but I think it mostly depends on circumstances."

"I know one thing. If they catch me now, they'll kill me. These people talking on the news are trying to frighten other people and trying to make them hate me. And they feel disgust. They keep talking about 'alien intelligence' and 'animal instincts'."

"They won't catch you. As long as you're careful."

"They have to get close to do it. Last time, they shot me with a dart while one of them was talking to me. A little arrow filled with anaesthetic. But now if anyone tries to get close, I'll grab him and hold him in front of me. And afterwards I'll kill him, so he can't tell where I live."

"Don't do that. Knock him out, and we'll gag him and keep him here until you can get home. Then we'll let him go."

"It might be a good idea to have a hostage if we drive through Mexico."

"More trouble than it's worth. We'd have to keep our eye on him all the way. I don't like the idea of hostages, anyway. It's so cowardly. It's so like what they did to you."

"What we should really have as a hostage is a baby. Nobody would try to shoot us with darts if we held it up in front of us upside-down."

Dorothy set down her fork and held her hands over her face. She told him about her two children again, this time in more detail. She started to cry. He patted and hugged her, and crooned in her ear.

"I don't dislike them," he said. "I would like to see one. I've seen them on television. It would be interesting. Could you bring me one to look at?"

"Larry, darling," she told him, "they don't just hang around street corners or something. Babies belong to people. The only time they're ever left alone is if the mother is so weighed down by shopping bags that she has to park the baby nearby in its push-chair, but just for a few seconds. Those are the only cases of baby-stealing I've heard of."

"So they are stolen? What for?"

"Lonely women. I used to think about it myself sometimes. For a few months. I'd see them outside the supermarkets and think: see how much they care for you—you'd be better off with me, I wouldn't leave you unprotected and ignored like that."

"We could borrow one."

"They cry. And we'd have to put it back."

"We could just let it go and it would find its own way home."

"Babies aren't like other small animals. They're helpless."

"All of them? How peculiar."

"They're very slow to develop, and almost everything they develop has to be taught. If you don't know how to teach it, or don't bother to, they never learn it."

Dorothy cleared the table and brought in coffee.

"Where you come from, are the births one at a time, or a number all together?"

"Both. It depends. Sometimes one way, sometimes the other."

"It's the same here. There can be two, three, four, five, but the most common is just one. The higher the number, the more unusual it is. But, I'm sure it used to be the other way around. A long time ago."

"Do you think that you and I—"

"I was just wondering about that this afternoon. I'd be delighted if it happened."

"Are you sure? It might put you in danger. And any child or half-child of mine would be called a monster, wouldn't it?"

"Born on American soil to an American mother—such a child could become President. It would be American. And I'm married so it would also be legitimate. After I sold the story to the dailies, it would be rich, too. It's surprising how little people mind what they're called, so long as they have enough money."

"A mixing of the species is said to produce a sterile offspring, isn't it?"

"The only one I know about is mules. But I don't think it holds true with plants. I should look it up. With you and me, we're so alike I'm not sure if we should really be called separate species. We might be the same species at different branches on its evolutionary development."

"At the Institute, they said I was a different species. Even Professor Dexter said it. So we might not mix."

"That doesn't surprise me. They didn't like you and they treated you shamefully. They'd want an excuse. For centuries people like that kept saying women didn't have souls. And nearly everyone still believes it. Same thing."

"The soul I know about. Professor Dexter was very interested in that. He said it was the reason why he chose to study science."

"I knew a girl once," Dorothy said, "who was stolen by a monkey when she was a baby. Dull girl. That was her one big moment of drama, before she was old enough to appreciate it. Her mother was in the hospital in Africa with her, a newborn baby, and the window was open. Outside the window was a big tree, and the tree was full of monkeys climbing up and down the branches. Suddenly one of the monkeys came in through the window, picked up the baby, and ran out again into the tree. It sat on a branch, rocking the baby and looking back at the women all screaming in their beds. Her mother was frantic, of course. I never learned how they managed to get her back."

"They were frightened the monkey would take her away and bring her up like a monkey?"

"They were probably scared it would drop her. Young monkeys automatically cling to the mother's fur. It might have slung the baby around its neck and jumped for a branch, thinking the baby would grab on tight. Anyway, they must have gotten her back somehow, because she was there to tell the story. She did tell me, too, only I'd forgotten till just now. She seemed to think it had been such an amazing event, but that presupposes a belief that she was so much better than a monkey. And who's to say? To herself, of course, but that isn't a test of anything, ever, except to your own self. It's like saying people don't have souls, when all you mean is you're not interested."

They went swimming together and made love on the beach. Dorothy still felt like a teenager. At the time when her hope and youth and adventurousness had left her, she had believed herself cheated of those early years when nothing had happened to her, although it might have. Later still, she realized that if she had made an effort, she herself could have made things happen. But now it didn't matter. Here she was.

They dried themselves off, drove around for a while, and walked through some of their favourite gardens in bare feet. Dorothy was less nervous than the first time they had gone out, but she still felt a sense of possible danger and an edginess, which she was beginning to enjoy. She skipped and danced after Larry, as with his long legs he went loping down the length of the flowerbeds. She giggled with nerves.

They found a back garden where there was a goldfish pond. The house next door had a bamboo grove, in the middle of which garden chairs and couches were set out. Dorothy stretched out on the plump cushions of a sofa. Larry sat next to her at the foot. She looked up at the stars. It was a warm night.

"I don't know how they'd get all this in if it rained," she said. "Maybe they just grab the pillows and let the frames get wet."

Larry asked her about the stars, which she didn't know much about. He had seen a television programme about them. They both looked up for a long time in silence. A breeze rustled in the bamboo.

He said, "They are real, aren't they? Not just pictures?"

"Of course they're real."

"How do you know? It's one of the things I find hard to understand; so many things are pictures. You watch pictures, but then you see the thing, and it's a picture, too."

"Well, I can't prove they're real, but they're so far away that it would take millions of years to get to them."

"Maybe not. Maybe it only looks like that. It could be just a reflection."

"I don't know enough about it to explain it. You should talk to an astronomer. Doesn't the TV programme tell you?"

"Maybe they're lying."

"Why?"

"They lie about lots of things. Remember the cornflakes." The cornflakes, kept for Fred, who sometimes liked them for breakfast, had made Larry throw up. While Dorothy had cleaned up after him, he had taken a bite out of the box and said he preferred the box to the stuff inside it.

She laughed. They put their arms around each other. He asked, "Do you do this with Fred?"

"Not for a long time now. Nearly two years. We used to. Then all the other business started. You know, what I told you about. And after a while, everything had changed."

*   *   *   *   *

*T*he next morning, Larry was standing in the living-room, watching Dorothy vacuum the rug and taking an occasional turn with the nozzle, when the doorbell rang.

Dorothy switched off the machine and raised her head. Suddenly she remembered.

"Mr Mendoza. Quick, get back into your room and lock the door."

Larry fled towards the kitchen in large, easy leaps. Dorothy waited a few seconds, then opened the door.

Mr Mendoza stood on the path, looking to the side, as though he couldn't make up his mind whether to ring again or go away. Dorothy smiled.

"Thank you for the note. I'm sorry I wasn't in. Shall we go through the list now?"

Mr Mendoza smiled back and dipped his head. He was a quiet, charming man, slow in all his movements and with a facial expression of relaxed steadiness. Dorothy had liked him from the beginning. He had come to work about a year after Bingo was run over, and it had been a help to be with someone and not be expected either to make conversation or to respond to it. It was still like that. She knew a little about his family, but when they talked, it was usually about plants and flowers, and they still called each other by their last names, like people of her grandmother's generation. At some point, just as she had thought of suggesting that they drop the formality, she had realized that he took it as a sign of respect.

Mr Mendoza gestured towards the far corner of the garden, up against the fence. He touched the brim of his hat and said something about the dangers of insecticide. Dorothy nodded. One of the reasons why Mr Mendoza was going through a period of great popularity was that in addition to being honest, sober, hardworking and punctual, he avoided chemicals. And one of the reasons why he remained loyal to Dorothy when other people were clamouring for his expert care and probably offering him huge salaries, was that she listened to what he said, was interested in it, deferred to his judgement and asked his opinion about things she had read or heard. Nor did she forget what he told her. She was a good gardener herself now, because he had been her teacher.

They discussed vegetables and compost. Dorothy asked if he'd like to come in for a cup of coffee, but he regretted that he had to go see Mrs Henderson. She said that she understood the regret: she had once met Mrs Henderson. Mr Mendoza chuckled quietly. He raised his hand in a lazy wave as he went down the path.

She looked in on Larry, finished the vacuuming with him, and watched a television programme. He liked to have her with him to explain things. On some days when she came home from shopping, he would ask one question after another. The only programme he enjoyed as entertainment rather than information was one peopled by puppets. The puppet she liked best was the wild one with all the teeth; his favourite was the saxophone player.

One day she had come home to find him doing an imitation of something. "What is it?" he asked her, but she couldn't understand what he was doing: punching, stalking, listening, fighting, twitching, acting all at once. He wouldn't tell her what it was supposed to be. It was the first question she had failed to explain since her collapse over the subject of industry and progress. She had started out with the introduction of agriculture, the coming of industry, the exploitation of women, the fact that it all started in the home where there was no choice, the idea that eventually robots and machines would release people to live a life of leisure and explore their own personalities; but, just before she reached that point, she forgot how to wind it up. A friend of Estelle's had once mapped it out for her so that it all sounded so clear, but now she couldn't remember just how it went. Even what she could recall didn't seem to make so much sense any more. In fact, it was sort of a mess and impossible to explain. She had stopped, confused, and added, "But what people really want is to be happy."

She had a cup of coffee and made Larry an early lunch. As she was drying her hands on a paper towel, the phone rang. Estelle was at the other end with a breathless story of how Sandra had the car and could Dorothy bring hers instead.

"Yes, sure. See you soon," Dorothy said, and hung up. She talked about Estelle, and said that Estelle was the one person she would like Larry to meet, but that she just couldn't take the chance.

"Better not," he agreed, as he sliced an avocado into the salad bowl. "We need some more of these."

On the way to Estelle's house, she bought another large bag of avocados. The man in the grocery store said, "Giving a party?" and she nodded. They weren't cheap either. In a little while, Larry's presence would begin to show on the food bills after all. Perhaps, if she and Larry hadn't become lovers straight away, she would have had an ally. Fred would have been the natural person to turn to for help. She might have been able to tell him about Larry. She thought about it, and decided that maybe even now it wasn't too late.

Estelle came to the door all dressed up. Dorothy said, "Est-elle, are they going to be filming the audience?"

"It's for my ego, dear. Drive on. I'm sorry about the mix-up with the arrangements. We're going to have to go in your car all the way, I'm afraid. Sandra's getting impossible about how much she needs the car."

"How about Stan and Charlie—think they might be there?"

"If it was sportscars, maybe. Not dresses."

The day was beginning to warm up. It was going to be like a summer day. Estelle put on a pair of dark glasses against the glare. Dorothy hummed as she drove.

Out at the studios, the parking was crowded even though they were early, but inside the buildings there was room to move. Dorothy was looking at the other people, most of them women, who wandered in small groups from one large glass case to another. And so it was that her attention was not really fixed on any one object when suddenly something seemed to loom in front of her. Like an animal that was showier than the peacock, and raised up as if riding in state from the safety of its glass box, a dress displayed itself to her. It was tiered, arranged in lacy scallops, pleated folds, glittering swags, and appeared to be made of solid gold. Inside, presumably helping to hold it upright, stood a woman-shaped white china dummy. But the dummy was nothing; the dress was everything. There had been no face painted on the blank head, but a powdered wig had been placed on top.

Estelle said, "No wonder they had a revolution, huh? Think of the cost of that thing. And this one's only a copy."

"It must have kept a lot of people in work."

"Come on. Wouldn't you rather be the one to wear it than the one to make it?"

"Oh, sure. I didn't mean that. Anyway, I read somewhere that these cost almost as much as the originals would have. They are amazing, aren't they? It changes your whole idea of what a dress should be for. It would have been like walking around in your own little silk house."

"Nothing below the waist, that was the idea. Women were such pure creatures. From the waist down, they were just a flow of brocade. And they didn't wear underwear, either."

"It must have been cold. Especially without central heating. They must have worn something in the winter."

"I can't imagine living in a different time," Estelle said. "Not in the future, and certainly not in the past. Can you?"

"I'll tell you something even harder to imagine," Dorothy said, thinking about Larry. "Can you think what it would be like to live in a different world?"

"Like Bel-Air, you mean?"

"No, not this world. A different one."

"In the future?"

"Any time. Like science fiction. Where the people look sort of like you, but not quite the same."

Estelle laughed. "Little green men?"

"Big green men," Dorothy said. She caught sight of two more dresses in their glass cases: one white, like a wedding cake, the other black. She thought suddenly of the days when gentlemen and ladies assembled in such clothes to dance the minuet, and how Larry might look among such a company; large, dark-green and handsome, bowing to a woman in a layered dress and dancing with a strong, springy step.

"My God," Estelle whispered, "there's Charlie. And look what he's got with him. A sixteen-year-old red-head."

"Where?"

Estelle pointed the pair out to Dorothy, and led her behind the black dress. Charlie and the girl were moving away, their backs towards the two women.

Dorothy said, "I think they're heading for the exit."

"The bastard."

"How do you know? Maybe it's his daughter."

"How many girls like that do you know who hold hands with their fathers in public and look goo-goo-eyed at them?"

"I think you're probably right."

"I bet he's told her he's a producer. I wouldn't put it past him. I wouldn't put it past any of them."

"But now you're free to do the same thing. Never mind. I'm sorry, Estelle. It isn't nice, is it?"

They moved on to a grey dress covered in sparkling jewels.

"Well, it's a bit of a kick in the teeth," Estelle said. "If only I'd played around like that when I was young."

"And you'd have gotten impotent men in their fifties wanting to get back at their wives and doing it through you. You had all that time in highschool with the boys."

"I bitterly resent all that wasted time. And what I resent most of all is that the ones I did get never, never looked like the Greek statues."

"The Greek-statue types may have been too busy going out with other boys to notice you."

"In a way. They were usually just too busy playing football and getting drunk. They didn't bother much about any of us."

"Look at this." Dorothy stopped in front of an embroidered jacket. "I thought this was going to be just the dresses."

"No, all the costumes. I wonder if they're going to sell some of them off, like that sale last month."

"Thinking of buying one?"

"Mmm." Estelle moved to a case containing another white dress. This one looked as though it had been sprinkled with shimmering dots of some kind, little twinkling bits of jewels. The past months' sales of dresses out of the studio wardrobes had included evening gowns that had been designed in the thirties and forties and could still be worn nowadays, but these— even at a costume party, they would stand out.

"Estelle, you aren't serious?"

"It would be a hell of a thing to own, wouldn't it?"

"But where would you wear it? In the kitchen while you were opening the cat food?"

"Dotty, sometimes you are just so unromantic, I can't understand it. If we all only owned the things we needed! You don't understand the nature of desire."

"I do," Dorothy said. "I do now. But I wasn't talking about that. I was talking about how you'd look sort of sitting somewhere eating a sandwich in a dress like a box. In the first place, how would you sit down?"

"Slowly," Estelle said. "Let's see what they're giving us to eat."

They had just finished two rounds of sandwiches and a cup of coffee, and were going back to get a few more sandwiches, when a man in front of them who was trying to go in the opposite direction, said, "Hi, Estelle."

"Oh, hi," she answered. They passed each other. As Dorothy reached the table, Estelle turned and looked backwards. She said, "Let's go."

"You don't want the sandwiches?"

"Oh, all right." Estelle grabbed some of the sandwiches, put them into a paper napkin, and moved down the table. "That was Stan," she said.

"Oh. He looks nice."

"And so did the woman he was with. Jesus, both of them in the same afternoon. Isn't there anything else going on in town but they've got to bring them here?"

When they were sitting in the car again, Dorothy turned the key and said, "But they still don't know about each other, do they? And now you wouldn't have to feel guilty about that, if you ever did. And you don't know what relationship they have with those women."

"Hah!"

"Anyway, they keep going out with you. And they wouldn't if they didn't like you."

"Maybe I'm just Tuesday or Friday, like handkerchiefs, or those sets of underpants with the days of the week sewn on them."

"Not really?"

"A girl I went to school with had a set."

"How do you know?"

"She told me. As a matter of fact, she showed me. I was so impressed. She said the writing was in a different colour for each day. She'd been given them for her birthday."

Dorothy was happy as she drove along the highway under the blue sky. She thought about Larry. She hummed again.

Estelle said, "I feel pretty terrible."

They had coffee at Estelle's house. Dorothy tried to comfort her, but Estelle was more interested in thinking up some plan of revenge.

"I suppose," Dorothy said, without thinking, "you could hire somebody out of central casting and pretend he was your latest."

"That's an idea."

"I was joking. And wouldn't that drive them away?"

"I don't think so. I've told you already, they want to get married. Hah! Get married to me, and go out with their fancypants girlfriends."

Dorothy clicked her tongue and shook her head. She looked over the edge of her coffee cup and said that on the other hand, Estelle had been two-timing them both from the beginning, hadn't she?

"Oh, that's different."

"Oh, uh-huh. How's it different?"

"That's just like insurance, that's all. In case one of them quit on me. I wasn't the one who kept asking to get married. That's what makes it so horrible. They've got to have somebody to do all their domestic drudgery full-time, and substitutes when the fancy one is out with somebody better."

"Maybe it would make you feel better to find a third one for a while."

"Maybe it would make me feel better to have a drink. Want one?"

"No, thanks."

"I still think your idea about phoning up central casting is a pretty good one."

"And if you had one of those dresses, you could probably hide him under it. Weren't they something? It would be like wearing another personality, a dress like that."

"I don't think I could take any more personality. Maybe I should forget about the dress. Anyway, it would only look right if you had the right hairdo. You'd need one of those powdered wigs."

"They were pretty. They didn't look as stiff as the ones in the pictures. But I can't stand the idea of something pressing on my head like that. I don't know how actresses and dancers can wear wigs all the time."

"Have a drink, Dorothy. Don't let me drink alone."

"So there'll be two drunks instead of one."

"Who said anything about drunk? Just a couple of—"

Dorothy stood up. "Estelle," she said, "you don't need it. You don't need it."

Estelle sighed. She put the bottle back in the cupboard. Dorothy picked up her car keys and purse. They walked to the door.

"In five years, you'll laugh about it," Dorothy said.

"Sure. But not now."

"Just ask yourself if you want to go on seeing them or not. And then act according to that. O.K.?"

"Thanks, Dotty."

"Any time. Thanks for the show. You still want to do that matinée?"

"I don't know. I may have to take Sandra in for an interview. I just don't know the day yet. Call me up."

Dorothy changed direction on the way to the main road. She drove back to town and then went on to the museum gardens, parked the car and walked around, looking at the trees and flowers. There were two old women being pushed in wheelchairs by uniformed nurses. Me, one day, she thought. And between now and then, nothing that can be done to avoid it, except an earlier death. But the gardens were pleasant. The grass in particular was luxuriantly green and well kept. She wondered if Larry would like to come here.

There was no fence, which meant that they could get in easily, but also that other people could, too. They might run into a gang of beer-drinking rowdies with switchblades. It was probably better to stick to the beach and maybe that garden with the bamboo grove.

She drove home, to find Fred there early. He said, "I've got to go out to a meeting." She nodded. On the stairs he turned. "What have you got in that bag?" he asked.

"Oh, more avocados, of course," she said, as if joking, and went through the door into the kitchen. A few minutes later, she heard him running down the stairs. He called out a goodbye and the front door slammed. Suddenly she went back to the living-room and looked out the window. She saw him getting into a car parked at the kerb. No one else was in the car; he must have hired it.

She had an early, leisurely dinner with Larry. They ate in the kitchen and listened to some music turned down low. The programme finished while they were still eating, so Dorothy switched it off and afterwards they talked. She told him about the fashion show and about Estelle meeting Charlie and Stan.

He said, "Is this important?"

"I don't know. It's just something that happened today, so it's part of my life to talk about."

"Your friend Estelle thought it was very important?"

"Yes, she certainly did. She was upset. Not as much as she sounded, but quite a lot."

"Why?" he asked, launching Dorothy into an explanation of the mating habits of human beings. She wasn't even sure that she was right about half her pronouncements. Every time Larry asked a question, she felt less sure. They seemed to be sensible questions, and she wondered why she had never thought of them herself. Then, at one point, he said, "For us, it's easier. Only the female is wanting and jealous and so on during mating, and the one she wants is the strong one. If you aren't strong, she stops wanting you and there is no mating."

"But would you go to a different female if you couldn't get the one you wanted?"

"Of course."

"And would you be as happy with her as you would have been with the first one?"

"I don't know. It is important?"

Dorothy was nonplussed. He also said, "When we want something, it's true. We don't want something we can't have and not like the thing we get instead. The thing you want is the thing you have, isn't it?"

"No," Dorothy said. "Not at all. You should know that. What about prison? You were in one. And there are all kinds of prisons in the world. Everywhere."

Larry stood up, pushed his chair in to the table, and did the strange, contorted movements again, asking, "What is it?"

"I don't know. I told you. Is it a joke?"

"I don't know either, that's why I'm asking you. I saw it on TV."

"Oh, no wonder. Well, I'll watch with you. Maybe I can catch it on another day." She tried to establish a time for the programme. Larry said he thought that it was an ad of some kind.

As soon as it grew dark, Dorothy drove them out in

the car. They went to the beach again and swam, and talked. She told Larry about the museum park and he said that it sounded nice. Dorothy was sorry that she had brought the subject up.

"It's much too dangerous. If anything happened, we'd be too far away from the car."

"Let's go see."

"All right, I'll drive past. But that's all. We won't get out of the car."

She skirted the museum grounds on one side and across the front. Shadows of palm trees hung patterned across the way in front of them as Dorothy turned the wheel again. Larry leaned out of the window, breathing in.

"At the back, the lawns slope down to the sea. It's a beautiful view. I don't know how they manage to keep the grass and gardens so healthy with the salt air."

"Can we stop here, please?"

She pulled over to the side of the road, stopped the car, and turned off the gas. From a distance they could hear the ocean, almost seeming to echo or imitate the sound of cars on the roads nearby. There was a tiny chirping of insects and the warm air was made fresh by night gardens.

"We can walk a little," Larry stated. He opened his door. Dorothy reached back, throwing her arm around his neck and shoulders.

"Please," she said. "I'm nervous about it." He detached her arm, got out, shut the door softly, and came around to her side. "You come, too," he said.

She followed him on to the immense stage of grass where the silhouetted trees and bushes leaned out into the air like the shapes of boats in a harbour. Dorothy wanted to dodge from one protecting shadow to the next, but Larry pulled her along into the open, holding her by the hand and carrying his sandals in his other hand.

He made her prowl around the grounds for a full twenty minutes, asking her questions about the museum when she thought it would be safer not to talk. Once, a car turned the corner on the road and Dorothy pulled her hand away and jumped behind a large bush as the headlights arched across the road. Larry came after her, unhurried, and saying, "The lights would not shine this way. Or is it some other reason you're hiding?"

"No, that was the reason."

He made her take one more turn around the palm avenue, and then agreed to go back to the car. He said, "I like this place."

"I do too, very much. But I think we've been damn lucky not to run into anybody. Please, let's not take any more chances like this, Larry."

"You are too frightened. It spoils your enjoyment."

"Larry, you're all I've got," she said.

He spread his arms out away from the car to take in the earth and sky all around, and said, "You've got all this. And you live here. It's your home."

Dorothy sat behind the wheel and drove silently for about five minutes. Then she tried to explain to Larry that "all this" wasn't much good without another person to share it with. He said that people were everywhere, there were millions of them; she said that people were all different and you had to find the ones who fitted with you. He said that he didn't understand that. How were people different? "Inside," she said, which mystified him, and when she asked if all the people where he came from were exactly the same, he said yes. When she told him that she couldn't believe it, he made a further statement: "We all do the same things, so we are the same. Here you all do different things."

Dorothy thought about that. She said, "If that were really true, men would be more different from other men than women from other women, because men's jobs are very varied, while most women do the same things. But it isn't true—women differ from each other just as much as men do. Do you think we could trust some other people to help us?"

"No," he said quickly.

"If they were other housewives like me? Just like me?"

"No. You are right. It's perhaps more complicated than I thought at first."

"And you don't really mean where you come from everyone is just like you."

"Oh, yes. That part's true."

*   *   *   *   *

*F*red asked Dorothy to come to an office party the next week. That was unusual enough, because he himself never liked that kind of thing. They sat on the sidelines in someone's house, with plates balanced on their knees. People were dancing to records and everyone said how nice it was to meet again. It was a very dull party. A few days later, he wanted to take out a visiting client and his wife, and have Dorothy come along. They went to a good seafood restaurant and had a pleasant evening. It was almost like old times. As they were leaving, Dorothy noticed the Cranstons sitting down at a special large table set for about twenty people. Jeanie Cranston jumped out of her seat to say what a surprise, and they must get together more often. Dorothy said yes, of course, but she knew they wouldn't. For years now they had really only been friends through Estelle. Dorothy took a quick look at the crowd they were with: loud, overdressed, yelling at each other across the table. Joshua looked the way Estelle had described him—smug, pompous and somehow not right.

The next morning before lunch, while Larry was peeling potatoes with her, Dorothy had a telephone call from Estelle. It was a distress call. She sounded drunk, and though what she seemed to be talking about was some dangerous characters her daughter Sandra was keeping company with, Dorothy was sure that the real trouble had to do with Charlie and Stan. She said she'd drop over in the afternoon.

"Start gargling with Listerine," she added, "and be careful not to swallow any, because if you're drunk when I get there, I'm turning right around and going home again. I might even phone up Charlie and Stan and tell them about each other."

Estelle screeched with laughter and hung up.

Larry helped to start off a new crop of apple cucumbers, he made the salad for lunch, and did the dusting while Dorothy vacuumed. Then he helped her to clean the silver—what there was of it—which she always forgot until she caught sight of a blackening cream jug in the corner of the top cupboard or a ladle at the side of the middle drawer.

She looked over to where he was, seated at the other end of the kitchen table in the light which, since his arrival, she had blocked by curtains because of his sensitive eyes. He concentrated on polishing spoons with a silver cloth: six teaspoons from a great-aunt. One leg was slung over the other, which would have looked strange enough, but he was also wearing a flowered apron fastened around his waist, and it contrasted stunningly with his large, muscular green body, his nobly massive head. Dorothy thought he looked, as always, wonderful. And his hands, in spite of their size and strength, were nimble and delicate in all their movements. He said that he enjoyed housework. He was good at it, and found it interesting. It was so different from anything he had known before: the hands had to be kept in constant motion, while the rest of the body remained more or less still.

They were lying in bed and watching television that afternoon, when Larry said sharply, "Look!"

"What?"

"What is it?"

"Where?"

"On the screen."

"Oh, it's an ad for a dance company."

"But what is it? Look."

"It's somebody called Merce Cunningham. You were right—it's an ad, for a dance programme coming up next week. It's a series. He has a dance company of his own."

"What's he doing?"

"Dancing."

"No, no, no," Larry said, getting out of bed, standing on the floor, and doing the strange motions he had been doing for days now. Suddenly Dorothy realized that he was giving a perfect imitation of the dance.

"That's his dance," she said.

"But what is it? What does it do?"

"I don't think it does anything. It expresses some emotion or idea, or gives an impression of an event. It makes variations with patterns. Do you like it?"

"I don't understand it," he said, getting back into bed.

"It's too bad I can't take you to see things. You should see some classical ballet, then I could try to explain from there."

"I've seen it," Larry said. "I can understand that."

"Really? You liked it?"

"Yes, very nice. Full of music."

"So is this."

"Not the same."

"No," Dorothy said. Most of the time, if she couldn't explain something to him straight away, he didn't push it. The last time she'd been stuck was when he said he didn't understand "radical chic".

Later in the afternoon, she drove over to Estelle's. Just before she rang the bell, she had a feeling that no one was at home. She rang three times. No answer. She walked around to the back and peeked into the kitchen.

Estelle was sitting down at one side of the booth-and-table across from the stove, and Sandra was in the middle of the room, shouting. Dorothy could hear her right through the window: "—stupid old ... never ... bitch ... all the time ..."

Dorothy rapped on the glass with her car keys. Sandra looked up, her face heavy, mask-like and intent. Then she disappeared. Next to Dorothy the kitchen door was flung open.

She walked in. Sandra was just going out the door that led to the dining-room. Estelle hadn't moved. Dorothy sat down at the other side of the table.

"How bad is it?"

"What?" Estelle asked.

"The hangover."

"I've got a hangover, all right. I've got a hangover from living forty-four long years."

"How old is Sandra now, anyway? I always forget. Is she fifteen?"

"Sixteen. They're all doing it at twelve now. She's been on the pill for two years. Well, I told you."

"But she's going through phases very fast. She'll probably get through a lot of unsuitable people before she settles down."

"Unsuitable," Estelle said.

"Isn't it better to have her experiment around than go all starry-eyed and get into a marriage that's going to break up in a couple of years? Then she'd be back where she is now, except maybe she'd have a child to bring up, too."

"If she were married, at least it might prove he loved her."

"Oh, Estelle. Do you love Stan, or Charlie?"

"She's trying to get back at me through this."

"Maybe," Dorothy sighed. She waited for Estelle to launch into explanation or self-justification, but she just sat slumped against the wall.

After a long while, Estelle said, "What a mess. I'm sorry I got you out here. I'm not very good company and I don't really know what to do about this. I don't want her to get hurt, but if I give her her head, there could be other people who get hurt."

"Who is this boy?"

"A man. Our age."

"My God."

"Oh, yes. You're beginning to see, now."

"I guess we're lucky it isn't Stan or Charlie. Or is it?"

"Not quite." Estelle rubbed her hands over her face and sat up straight. "Coffee?" she asked.

"Just a little. And if I can't help, let's change the subject. Tell me about Joey."

"That isn't changing the subject so much. He's developed some kind of knight-errant complex about it. *My sister must be pure* type of thing. That's how I found out. They've been fighting about it for days, till last evening it all came out what the trouble was."

After the first cup, Dorothy wanted to go, but it was just at that point that Estelle decided to tell a little more of the story about Sandra.

"Have you seen this man?" Dorothy asked.

"Oh, I don't want to talk about it."

Estelle went on to say that she didn't know what to do, because every move she made was being misinterpreted by her daughter. She had the feeling that the girl was just waiting for her to put a foot wrong.

"This man—" Dorothy began.

"The thing is, I've always tried to bring them up to compensate for the way I was brought up."

"Well, all mothers do that."

"And now it's all paying off. What really kills me is this idea that a lot of it goes back to the divorce. Punishing me for it."

After the second cup of coffee, Dorothy got away. She was less worried about Estelle than when she had heard her voice over the telephone, but wasn't very optimistic about how long she would stay sober. As long as things didn't reach a crisis during the time when she would have to be driving Larry to safety, she ought to be able to deal with everything.

Fred wasn't home yet when she arrived. She went into the kitchen, looked in on Larry briefly, and as soon as she heard the car, walked into the living-room.

"What now?" he said, taking off his jacket. He put it over the back of a chair.

"Talk. Our famous talk we were going to have. About Suzanne and the vacation, and everything."

"I've got to go out. Can't we do all that later?"

"It's always later. One day it's going to be too late."

He looked at her over his shoulder, but said nothing. She thought: he was going to say, "It's already too late," but he changed his mind.

"Well, what do you think?" he said. "But make it quick."

"I thought we might try the separate vacations again, and get Suzanne to come afterwards. But I'm going to need some help with her this year. I can't stand it much longer."

"Yes. All right."

Nothing would happen, of course. Every year she said the same thing about Suzanne.

"So shall I call up Suzanne and tell her?" Dorothy asked.

"Yes, O.K."

"Are you really listening?"

"Of course, of course. I'm just in a hurry. I've got to go out."

Dorothy picked up the telephone and dialled Suzanne's number. Fred went upstairs. Suzanne, as Dorothy had hoped, was in the middle of preparations for dinner; in fact, she was giving a party and sounded disorganized.

"Who? Dorothy? Why don't I call you back when we can talk?"

"No, no. No need for that. It's just to say that we're going to have to make it after the twelfth."

"But that's ages away."

"I'm afraid it just won't work out any other way."

"But I'll be on vacation then."

"Well, I'm afraid we're going to be on ours before then."

"Maybe I can come before you go."

"No, that's just it. We've got people staying." Dorothy thought of a name quickly. Suzanne always wanted to know all the details of everybody's life, and never forgot any of them.

"Dorothy, we'll have to talk about it. I've really got to go now."

"That's all right. We don't have to talk about anything until after the twelfth. O.K.?"

"Yes, but—"

"I'll get in touch with you then. Goodbye."

"I'll call you," Suzanne said. "Goodbye."

Dorothy wrote down on the notepad by the telephone that Suzanne was not to come until after the twelfth. When Fred came running down the stairs, still tying his tie, she told him and he said, "Yes, yes."

"And I've written it down on the pad in case she calls. If she comes before that, I'm moving out and taking the car."

"All right, all right," he said.

"Where are you going in a tie?"

"I've got to rush. 'Bye."

He was out of the house and into the rented car before she could think of what she had been meaning to say. Now she had forgotten. She went back to the telephone, underlined two words on the pad, and continued on towards the kitchen.

She and Larry had supper, and were just settling down in front of the TV set when she heard what she thought was the front door. Larry turned off the set and told her that her husband had come back. She scrambled up off the bed, although she didn't believe it. Much more likely that there was a burglar.

She opened the door to the living-room without making a sound. Exactly in her line of vision sat Fred, his head in his hands. She approached the chair silently and stood near him. He sighed. He said, "Oh, damn." She put her hand on his shoulder and he jumped. She patted his back.

"What's wrong?"

"What did I say?"

"When?"

"Just now."

"Nothing. You said, 'Oh, damn'. Where were you?
What happened?"

"It's so hard to explain."

"That's all right." She sat down beside him.

He said, "Well, it's so stupid and miserable. I was
seeing somebody. I didn't even like her, but I was
bored. She was the one who started it all. I wouldn't
have thought of it otherwise. And now she says she's
going to make a big scene and tell you. So, that's it.
I'm sorry."

Dorothy kept her hand on his back. She said, "Never
mind. If she wants to talk to me, let her."

"I think it's just to hurt me, but I don't want it
hurting you. That's why—I mean, I'd rather not have
said anything."

I'll bet, Dorothy thought. And he probably thinks
I had no idea. Still, I too would rather not have known
so exactly. She sat still, moving her hand lightly over
the back of his shirt and wanting to ask, "What's she
like?"

"You don't love her any more?"

"Oh, I never did. That's what's so dumb."

"Well, don't worry. I'll be prepared if anything
happens."

He still looked pathetic. Perhaps he wanted to warn
her that if the other woman told her such-and-such,
not to believe it. Well, Dorothy thought, I have Larry.
I can afford to be forgiving.

"Are you going out again tonight?"

"No."

"We can play Scrabble and plan out what's going to happen with the vacations."

They ended up playing four rounds. Dorothy brought coffee and made him some sandwiches. He said, "This is beginning to look like a tournament," and she answered, "No, just 'people to people', but I'm winning."

"That makes it people to etymological mastermind."

Dorothy wrote down the score and looked over the letters in her rack. "We haven't played this in a long time."

"That's because you kept winning."

Dorothy almost said, "Or because you were always out at night." There were a few moments around quarter to eleven when she thought she sensed movement from the kitchen, which would mean that Larry was sneaking out to steal a car for the night. And, there was another point when she knew for certain that her husband had decided, all in the space of an evening and without consulting her, to put their marriage back where it had been several years ago, before the single beds.

As they went upstairs, Dorothy reminded him about Suzanne and repeated that she would leave the house if Suzanne came before the twelfth.

"We could take our vacation together," Fred said. "Something fancy, for a change."

"I think it might be a good idea to go ahead and do them separately. Have time to think about things and get together afterwards. You know what vacations are.

They aren't really connected to the rest of life. Like honeymoons."

"Sounds good."

"But you don't need to go away for that."

"Sounds better," he said.

In the morning, Fred was hardly out the door and Dorothy back in the kitchen, when Larry appeared before her. He said, "They're looking for me," and pointed to the radio. Dorothy switched on the volume knob and led him to a chair.

The announcer's voice sounded excited and happy, as if advertising something. It said:

Last night, after a lull of weeks, Aquarius the Monsterman struck again. Five young lives fell victim to the bloodlust of this creature, five families now mourn. Yesterday they hadn't a care in the world, now they know the sorrow of the bereaved. And we must also ask ourselves if it is right that alien life-forms should be brought back at great public expense to lay waste the flower of our citizenry.

"They came at me with broken bottles. One of them said, 'Hey man, look at the size of him. We'll do something about that, to begin with.' And then they were all around me, so I had to hit as fast as I could. I'm sorry, Dorothy. It's going to make it harder for you, isn't it?"

Dorothy made a gentle, hushing gesture with her hand. She listened to the radio. The rest of the broadcast described the "bloodlust killings" of five boys or men in the gardens of the museum, where they had been the other night. She listened to the end, and then switched it off.

"Were you hurt?"

"Where they hit me and kicked me, but they weren't able to use the bottles. Or the knives—two of them had knives—so, my skin isn't broken."

She ran her hand along his face. He pulled away as she touched the side of his jaw. If the dark green colour hadn't masked it, there would probably be a spectacular bruise to go with the swelling, like the time Fred got into the fight on the freeway with the driver from Kansas.

"I'll get you something for it."

"I already put a cream on it. I found it with the medicines. It said it was for contusions."

They spent the morning quietly until Mr Mendoza arrived. This time, he came in for a cup of coffee and talked about the news, and said that the television version now was that these young men were brave and patriotic and so on, but he had seen their pictures in the morning paper and recognized them as punks and troublemakers from good neighbourhoods, who had the money and the time to hang around getting drunk and taking drugs and beating up people who were poorer than they were and who were out on their own.

"That friend of yours," he said. "It will be sad for a while, but it's better the way it is, you'll see."

Dorothy didn't know what he meant. She was terrified that he might have meant Larry. Could he have seen Larry through a gap in the kitchen curtains? Mr Mendoza said goodbye and left before she could say anything or even think about it.

He might have been referring to something in the newspaper coverage which she had misunderstood.

But "your friend", if it was an allusion to Larry, would have meant that the police should have been at the house hours ago. Fred had taken the paper with him again; she hadn't even seen it.

She turned on the television set in Larry's room. He was pottering around the living-room, looking at magazines and books. The screen showed police and public officials. Occasionally there was a shot of one of the doctors or scientists who worked at the Institute. There were some interviews, which had been taped very early in the morning, and panel discussions about the nature of civilized man and the aggressive instinct. Dr Forest stressed the animal's intelligence, Professor Dexter talked about the original capture and why it would be so dangerous to approach such a creature without qualified professional help. The police and officials spoke of quick action, possible hiding places, eating habits. Without actually saying so, the presenters of the programme were managing to suggest that Larry had remained in the area because of the opportunities for eating people. Not one of the men interviewed thought it might be possible that Larry remained so well hidden because he had made friends with someone. That question was never raised.

But perhaps the police had told them not to mention it. On the other hand, if the authorities believed that, surely they would find Larry more quickly by asking members of the public to snoop around all the houses near them. Now that she thought of it, of course, it was extraordinary that he should have chosen her. Most single people don't live in their own separate houses, most married people are in and out of all the rooms of their house.

While she was watching, Larry came in and sat down on the bed.

"How can they say those things? I used to think it was only the people at the Institute who were like that, but they are everywhere."

Dorothy turned the sound down almost to nothing, and came over to where he sat.

"You don't like it that I killed these people," he said. "You think it's bad. But they would have killed me."

"I know they would. I don't think it's bad at all. I'm just disappointed that if anything goes wrong with the Mexican plan, we can't use the newspapers. Before last night, we could have told the truth about the men in the Institute, how they were torturing you for their own pleasure in addition to all the horrible experiments they thought were going to prove something useful— and we would have had the defence of a victim. But now, everyone's going to think these thugs and creeps acted in an understandable way. Everyone except me and somebody like Mr Mendoza, who has a mind of his own. People will think these boys acted the way they did because they were frightened. Of course, if they had been frightened, which they weren't, it would have been the fault of the TV and the papers. They've been whipping everybody up."

"They always do. About everything. I've been reading and I've been watching. I'll tell you something else: I understand now."

"What?"

He stood up and did the dance they had seen on television. To Dorothy it looked exactly as it had when he had copied it before.

"Now I understand," he said.

"Is it different?"

"Yes," he said, "for me." Dorothy was about to ask some questions concerning the dance when still photographs were put on the screen behind him. She was curious to see who the people were. Larry moved back beside her on the bed.

"There are the people in the park. Do they look the same?"

"Nothing ever looks like a picture. That's what picture means."

"But can you recognize them?"

They both looked. One picture, two. The names weren't given. Three; and then, at the fourth picture, Dorothy said, "That looks like Estelle's son, Joey. My God, I wonder if that was what Mr Mendoza meant."

"What?"

"If that's the same person, I know his mother. In fact, she's my best friend. You know, my friend Estelle. I'd better call her up."

She went into the kitchen and telephoned from there. Larry stood behind in the doorway, looking at her. All she got was a busy signal. It was true, of course, that pictures never looked like the real person, and this one would have been taken a long time ago, but it had been near enough to make her think she recognized it, even without a name.

"Larry," she said, "I think I'd better go see if I can find Estelle. I'm sorry to leave you."

"You don't like it that I killed him. Does it make it worse that you knew that one?"

"Yes."

"Why? To do a bad thing is the same from a stranger as from someone you know. Maybe it's worse from someone you know."

"But you make allowances for the people you know."

"I told you what happened. There were five of them, they tried to kill me, and they jumped on me without any warning. They were armed, and they were enjoying themselves. That Joey one, too. Aren't you going to make allowances for me as well as him?"

"I've known him since he was a baby. I've held him on my lap."

"You've loved me more than you ever loved him, haven't you?"

Dorothy fidgeted with the telephone cord. She nodded and sighed.

"What really worries you most, Dorothy? It isn't because of what I've done—I can see that now."

"I guess it's Estelle. From the beginning, we were just the opposite: our families, our characters, and our marriages. But we've always gotten along so well, like sisters. We've helped each other so much. Once or twice our lives were broken up so seriously that each one of us was nearly ready to go under—really. So, when something hits Estelle badly, it hits me, too. You can't imagine how she complains about her children, even when they're there in the room, but I know they're really everything to her. She just adores them. I don't know how she'll ever recover."

"You did," Larry said.

"Sometimes I wonder."

She drove out to Estelle's house, but there was no
answer when she rang the doorbell, and none when
she went around to the back and pounded on the door.
She got the notebook out of her purse, ripped out a
page, and wrote a short letter, which she folded up to
look like an envelope, and pushed it through the slot
in the door.

She drove in the direction of the museum. From a
long way off it was obvious that there were crowds of
people driving towards the place, so she changed her
mind and took the turning for the coast. She stopped
the car under a eucalyptus tree and sat looking out at
the ocean. She felt like crying; for Estelle at the moment
and Estelle in the future, and for herself in the past,
when Scotty died. She tried to think of what to do,
and to arrange plans for hiding Larry, comforting
Estelle, getting rid of Suzanne, taking the holiday alone
without hurting Fred's feelings, and getting Larry back
to his home. If I do this, she thought, it should take
one week, two weeks, but if I do this . . . She couldn't
attach any of her thoughts together for very long. She
would much rather have cried. What she did, however,
was to fall asleep, with her shoulder up against the seat
and her head near the window. She woke up after about
twenty minutes and drove back to Estelle's house,
where there was still no answer.

*   *   *   *   *

She went back home. Fred's rented car was parked

outside and he was in the living-room. He was reading a newspaper.

"Seen this?" he asked, as she passed in front of him. He crinkled the paper at her to show what he meant, but kept right on reading.

"I haven't seen any of them. You took the paper with you when you left. I saw something on TV, but they didn't give any names. Was it Joey?"

"Looks like him. I'm not surprised. He was probably so spaced out, the monsterman just gave him a push and he fell over."

"Why do you call him a monster?"

"Well, an eight-foot tall green gorilla with web feet and bug eyes—what would you call him? A well-developed frog? Not exactly an Ivy-league type, anyway.'"

"I've met plenty of Ivy-leaguers I'd call monsters. And his feet aren't webbed, or only a little. And neither are his hands. They only seem that way at first glance. And he isn't any eight-foot tall. Only about six-seven."

"How do you know?"

"I saw it on television. Pictures taken before he escaped."

"You know, some idiot of a woman is trying to get up a petition to say this monster has been inhumanly treated, and so on."

"She's right. He was."

"Oh, come on."

"How would you like to be tied down and given electric-shock treatments by force, and only given any food when they'd decided you were co-operating enough in one of their horrible experiments?"

"You sound just like this Mrs what's-her-name here —Mrs Peach. You two should get together."

"Maybe."

"Actually, I'm not so sure I believe there ever was a monster. Might just be some poor clone or hybrid they've been working on in the labs. Gave him too big a dose of some hormone and it sent him haywire; something like that."

They had a quiet dinner and talked about plans for the future. Fred agreed that they would take separate vacations. Dorothy realized from the start of the meal that he wanted to say something about having children, but he didn't dare. She thought: he really is hoping to go back to where we were, and thinks then everything will work itself out.

At midnight, Estelle telephoned. She sounded very calm, and tired. The newspaper story had been right: it had been a picture of Joey on the screen. Dorothy wanted to go see her straight away, but Estelle said no, to wait till the afternoon of the next day. "The man from the funeral parlour," she explained.

Mr Mendoza came around again the next day. They worked in the garden and talked about a new variety of rose that had been bred for one of the European flower shows: it was supposed to be blue—not the pale grey or lilac blue you could buy at the nurseries, but a genuine bright royal blue like the blue of a first-prize ribbon.

"I sure would like to have a cutting," he said.

"Is it real? I mean, would it breed true? It takes a long time to tell, doesn't it?"

"You just have to wait and see."

They finished work too late for Mr Mendoza to come in for a sandwich, so Dorothy said that they probably wouldn't see each other for a few weeks. He would be working at other houses in the neighbourhood, and after that, she would be on her vacation. He asked her to tell him the exact date when she knew, because then he would drop by to see that everything was all right while she was away.

She ate her lunch with Larry in his room. They only turned the television on for a few minutes to watch the news. Mrs Peach, looking—with her short, permed hair, extra-strength glasses and prim but firm expression—like a caricature of an anti-vivisectionist, gave a brief speech which Dorothy thought very sensible. She raised the point that the so-called monster had been held in captivity for several months, isolated from its own species and investigated or experimented upon by scientists. The general public had never been told what sort of animal this was. She also stated that until the capture, this creature had been unknown to the scientific world. The question of Human Rights, or just rights in general, was as important in this case as though the creature had come from outer space.

Dorothy said, "If only she had spoken up right at the beginning. It's good, but it comes a bit late."

"It's all too late now, I can feel it. Before, I only suspected. Now, I'm certain. People are too afraid now. In a way, I'm glad. If they catch me now, they won't try to tie me up or knock me out to take me back to the Institute. They'll just beat me to a pulp and say I was trying to eat them up. Even if I gave myself up, it's too late. Haven't you noticed—they keep calling me 'the killer'?"

"Yes, I know."

"It's all right. I'd prefer anything at all to going back to the Institute."

The afternoon came. Dorothy was not prepared to find Estelle sober, but as it turned out, Estelle did not even look as though she had been crying. What was worse, she looked like a different person. She was very quiet, sometimes sighing long sighs. She forgot where she had put things she'd just set down for a moment, and she talked in a calm monotone about the funeral arrangements and the other parents.

Of course, Dorothy thought, there were five of them. It was going to be a joint funeral. And, naturally, the press would be having a field day.

"I think Sandra's taking it very hard. You know, we haven't been on very friendly terms. She threw herself at the man I was . . . just to hurt me, but that's all over. Over for me, anyway. She's going to have to start finding out for herself now, what's right and what isn't. I can't tell you how empty the house feels, Dotty."

"Yes, I know. That's what it was like with Scotty. His toys, his clothes. Right at first, I kept thinking I heard his voice everywhere, coming from a different room, and I'd get up and walk into the next room just—you know, thinking none of it had happened at all. And then I'd realize again."

Estelle nodded slowly. Her face was like the outline of a box, with no expression whatever.

"Estelle, did the doctor give you some kind of pills or something?"

"Have you ever heard of a doctor who didn't try to shoot you full of drugs? I'm not sick. I'm bereaved. That means I've got to keep all my strength to get through. And if I'm full of drugs, my resistance is going to be destroyed, isn't it?"

"Yes, of course. That was one of the biggest mistakes they made with me."

"I know. I told you."

"One of the things that helped the most was talking to you. And then going to work. Have you been able to cry at all?"

"I've been trying not to. At least, I think that's what's going on."

"It might help."

"I'm afraid it wouldn't stop. Remember what happened to you. They almost had you in the loony bin. Once you're helpless, one of those bastards steps forward with a hypodermic and the curtain comes down on your life. You stay there and they give you massive doses of sedatives every day because you're easier to take care of that way. And then your brain is pretty much slugged into submission. No more chance to find your way out of your troubles, ever."

Dorothy said she agreed. Estelle had always felt like that about doctors, by which she meant male doctors— the women, apparently, weren't so bad. But Dorothy until her troubles, had not agreed at all. She had twice been into the hospital for minor operations as well as for Scotty, and had thought everybody was so kind and nice. Despite the boredom of waiting around, she had enjoyed being taken in to the workings of a new world. She had found it easy that nothing was expected of her, no act of hers could be a mistake, a neglect, or something she should feel guilty about. It was wonderful, she had thought, that there were experts who had dedicated their time and strength to such demanding work and who could put you right when you were in real trouble—broken, cut, bruised, scrambled up inside. Only much later did the realization of her helplessness contribute to a certainty that nurses, doctors, in fact the whole idea of medicine, had made her a victim. To her it had not brought healing. It had brought death where she was sure death had been avoidable. Her own doctor was still all right and she had one weapon against him: she could just not go, and phone to say she felt fine. But hospitals—whenever she thought about them now, she felt like a sacrificial bundle on a stone slab, with the priests whispering to each other over her head.

"Drugs," Estelle said. "Money and drugs, and that's the history of civilization."

Dorothy wondered if Estelle was still referring to doctors, or if something had come out about Joey taking drugs. She didn't want to bring up the subject herself. She asked when the funeral was going to be held. Estelle gave a deep sigh.

"Listen, don't be hurt, but I really don't want anybody to come. I think I can get through it by myself—just. But anything real would make me crack up. It's going to be a performance, you know. Television, everything. Three of those families have sold the serial rights to the papers, and you should see them. You've never seen such people."

"Didn't you know them before?"

"Of course not."

"But you knew the boys?"

"No. They were just a bunch of rough kids Joey used to hang around with when he was trying to act tough. God knows what they were up to. Stealing TVs and stereos and car radios, and selling them—who knows? That's the kind they were."

"Do you think they provoked this man, or monster, whatever he is? That they ganged up on him, maybe?"

"Monster? Oh, Dorothy, I don't believe there's any such thing. Some kind of crocodile got up on its hind legs and broke out of that institute, but you can bet the poor thing's dead by this time. Or probably crawled back to the beach and swam away."

"What do you think it was?"

"Oh, another gang, and they're keeping quiet."

"There are people who say they saw him."

"I bet there are. There are people who could see Moby Dick in Times Square. It sounds to me like a big fight. They all had bottles and knives. So if there was only one man, he'd have to be one of these karate champions. I guess that's possible, too."

Dorothy poured out a second cup of coffee for each of them. This is all my fault, she thought. I've given him shelter and now this has happened. If I'd taken him straight to a good lawyer, we could have worked out some sort of defence for killing those two keepers.

Estelle stared into her cup. She stirred the coffee with a spoon, although she hadn't put anything in.

"Charlie and Stan called me," she said. "That was nice."

"Very nice. So you've forgotten about them being with those girls at the fashion show."

"Oh, that. Unimportant."

"Which one of them was it that Sandra made the play for?"

"That was somebody else."

"My God, Estelle, you've got a new one?"

"Not new. Old. Before Stan and Charlie. Years. I always felt guilty about it, but I couldn't end it, and then I guess I didn't want it to stop. But it's stopped now, all right. Let's not talk about that."

"Has Sandra changed towards you now? I mean, has it brought you closer together?"

"Nope. I don't even know if she's going to bother to turn up for the funeral. And the way I feel now, I'm not sure I really want her around much."

The electric clock on the wall clicked as it sometimes did when the minute hand jumped forward. Dorothy said, "Anything I can do. You know. I'll leave it up to you to call me, but if you don't after a few days, I'll call you. All right?"

"Yes, fine. Thanks, Dotty."

"Try to keep eating the right things, and don't let them give you pills, or use any other depressants."

"The girl means hooch. Finally she comes out with it."

"And I mean it."

"I'd like to get away from everything. Just everything."

"That might not be a bad idea. You could start packing after the funeral, and I'd take care of the house for you. You think about it. Are you sure you don't want me to be with you when—"

"No. Thanks."

Dorothy stood up. She said, "Any time you want to change your mind or need to talk, just pick up the phone, or come over." She kissed Estelle on the cheek and left.

On the way home, she thought to herself that Estelle would never just drop in without warning, any more than she herself would. It hadn't been such a great offer of friendship: do feel free to call on me for help any time between four and six, or when I'm not likely to be in the bedroom with somebody, and certainly not before the twelfth.

And if I hadn't been hiding him, she thought again, it wouldn't have happened.

About ten blocks before the house, she noticed that she was driving directly behind Fred in his rented car. He gave no sign of realizing she was there. Where they both usually turned off to the left, he kept straight ahead until turning to the right. She followed.

She followed him for just over ten minutes. He pulled up at the kerb in a street like the one they lived on themselves, got out, and rang someone's doorbell. Dorothy couldn't see who answered. She waited for a few minutes, not long, and then he came back out, got into his car, and drove on. He had been carrying something in his hand—an office file, or something like that. So, it was business, not pleasure.

She drove home a different way, and saw the rented car there before her. Fred was in a hurry again, tying his tie at the last minute.

"Where are you going?"

"Just out to some people's. I don't think I'll be too long."

"They need you in a tie?"

"It makes a good impression."

"Nowadays?"

"They're that kind of people."

"Let me do that for you," Dorothy said.

"When have I never been able to tie my own tie blindfold? I had to do it in that school play, remember?"

"Haven't you had anything to eat?"

"I'll pick something up."

At the last minute, he turned and kissed her on the cheek, quickly and as if panicked. He was out the door almost immediately.

Dorothy went back into the kitchen. She sat down at the table and tried to think. All during the drive, she had been excited. She had expected to find something or someone. But there had been nothing. The house probably belonged to Art Gruber or someone else like that, who had taken home a report by mistake. And yet, she felt let down.

Larry came and stood beside her. It was the first time he had ever come out of his room on his own during daylight, rather than waiting for her to come tell him that it was all right.

"You shouldn't have come out alone," she said.

"I heard he was gone."

"But I could have had the lights switched on and only the gauze curtains. Somebody outside could have seen you."

"I saw there was no light on." He sat down in a chair opposite her. He took her hand.

Dorothy smiled. Whenever he took her hand, it made her happy. She had had an inkling of the sensation that very first time, when he had walked into the kitchen and she had handed him the celery. She kept smiling, but she thought: he's taken his own lead now —he no longer avoids risks.

"You are sad," he said.

She nodded. She told him about Estelle. "And the whole business about the funeral. We'll probably be able to watch it on TV. It'll be terrible."

"I'd be very interested to see it. You talk so much about your friend Estelle."

"But after that, it's really going to be hard for you. I don't think it's going to be safe for you to go out at night the way you've been doing. They might not expect to see you driving a car, but once they do, they'll realize. Once a thing is in the air, everyone sees it, even if it isn't there. It's an influence. Like the flying saucers: if one person has a big story about them, half a dozen do. That doesn't necessarily mean it's impossible that they've seen anything—it just means people are prepared to notice everything, once they've been alerted. Before that, they really don't see things much."

"You must decide," he said. Dorothy felt relieved. If he wanted to act on his own, there would be nothing she could do. And there was another matter: when he spoke about Fred now, there was a shade to his voice. It might just be that he was jealous, that he wanted to hurt Fred. He knew how easy it was to hurt people, and he certainly had reason to want to take revenge on humankind.

She said, "I think we're going to have to go sooner than we'd planned. Very soon. I'll have to think it out. In the meantime, it would be better to stay indoors."

"No, let's go out, please. I want to walk on the grass in the gardens and look at the flowerbeds. Please. We could go back to the place with the chairs and the stickbushes."

"Bamboo. But it's taking such a risk."

"I'm going to feel sick if I can't go out. I know it."

The telephone rang. Jeanie Cranston was calling to ask Dorothy if she knew anything about Estelle, since the phone must be off the hook and the doors were locked, and the curtains drawn. What Jeanie really wanted to know was what her own reactions ought to be—would it be all right to send a letter, a telegram, flowers? Dorothy told her to put a note through the door if she wanted to, to stay away from the funeral, and wait for Estelle to get in touch.

She ate an early supper with Larry. They took a lot of extra time over their coffee. He wanted to know all about the Cranstons. The more Dorothy told him, the more he seemed fascinated. What struck him as most interesting was the fact that although Dorothy and Estelle talked about the Cranstons being "friends", neither of them genuinely liked the couple.

"Is this usual?" he asked. After some thought, Dorothy said she figured it probably was.

She agreed to go to the bamboo grove. While they were washing up the dishes, she asked, "When you go back, will the others think you've changed much?

I mean, because you find all these things interesting: the Cranstons, and so forth. Will it make them think you've changed for the better, or just that you aren't normal any more?"

"It's different," he said. "They'll come near me to find out. It's like smell. What's important is that they should still know who I am. I think they will."

"If you stayed away for a long time, they might not recognize you?"

"Or other things could happen. My abilities could leave me. How to swim, how to stay under. I'm eating different things up here. My life is different, my way of using the food is different—what's that word?"

"Metabolism. Over a long period, maybe it would make a difference." And, she again thought, there was the possibility of picking up a human disease. She said nothing, but wondered if he had thought of that himself.

It was still light when she eased the car out on to the driveway and into the street. A lovely, warm night, full of promise and romance as she had dreamed about it in her teens and as the advertisements had promised and still promised, for her and for everyone else too.

"You are driving very slowly," Larry whispered from the back seat.

"It's so nice out. And it's still light. Shall we go down to the beach for a while?"

"No, to the bamboo place."

"But we're going to have to drive around till it gets darker."

"All right. The beach."

Dorothy drove the car to their usual place. She

leaned her head back. Larry ran his hands through her hair, then got out of the car and moved into the front seat beside her.

"You know, I think if anything happens," she said, "so that we're separated, or if anything goes wrong—"

"What?"

"—not that it will . . . anyway, it might be a good idea to plan to meet here. You'd have the ocean right there, so you could stay hidden for a while, couldn't you?"

"Yes, sure. A long time. Months."

"Right. And I'd show up around this time, maybe later. You'd hear the car and see the lights if you came out on to the beach."

"I'll remember."

They drove to the street of the bamboo grove, parked and got out. They ran across a neighbouring yard, halting in the shadow of a tree.

"Larry, I have a feeling."

"Lots of people."

"Lots of cars parked in the road. There must be a party somewhere near. It makes it so risky."

"Never mind. They'll be drinking." He took her by the hand and led her forward through the sweet evening air. They walked over the warm lawns together like the college couples she had followed in her youth with her schoolgirl friend, Joan. On perfect evenings, like this one, they had trailed courting couples for yards, for blocks, from one neighbourhood to another, wondering about whether the young lovers were really lovers, what they actually did with each other, and whether they themselves would ever be strolling along like that with a man.

"Voices," Larry said.

Dorothy heard nothing for a few moments. Then the sound of talk came to her, as elusive as a wind-carried scent from flowering trees in the spring. It seemed to be coming from all directions at once, then suddenly it was gone.

"Where do you think they are?" she whispered. Instinctively she had ducked down into a crouching walk.

"They sound like they're where we were before. That big house with the garden and the bamboos."

"Let's go, then."

"No, let's look." He pulled her along by the hand. The buzz of voices became clearer, louder, and at last fixed. Soon it was loud enough and clear enough for Dorothy to distinguish whole sentences flung up out of the babble. How people whooped when they got together, and on top of that there were the explosions of laughter or contradiction that involved groups of from three to eight voices. So many rhythms chased each other and scurried through the main rise and flow of sound.

"Is it like the sea?" she whispered. "All the changing sounds?"

"No. Not at all. But I like the thought."

Dorothy put her head up against his collarbone and kissed him. She still held his hand.

"Let's find the bamboo place and the garden sofas," he suggested.

"Too dangerous."

"Just to see if we'd be hidden from sight."

"Well—"

"You could even go out into the crowd and bring us food and drinks."

Dorothy began to giggle. She followed, convulsed by hysterical smothered laughter, as Larry led the way. She held her other hand over her mouth.

As they approached the bamboo grove, there was less light, and less noise. Dorothy's giggles stopped suddenly. She sensed a change more subtle than a threat of danger, but just as urgent. It was the kind of feeling you might get from an unexpected alteration of temperature. She squeezed Larry's hand.

He pulled up in front of her and stood still. They listened to the distant sound of the party, the nearby rustling of the bamboo, and then a faint sound of moaning. Dorothy was afraid. Someone out there in the shadows was hurt, but they couldn't help whoever it was without betraying their own presence.

Larry stepped forward. He seemed to intend going on, whether she accompanied him or not. He dropped his hold on her hand.

She dashed after him. And all at once her eyes were used to the changed light. It wasn't really very dark at all. Certainly it was light enough to see the two people—the man almost fully dressed, the girl naked— who face to face were using the garden sofa so athletically and rhapsodically that before Dorothy realized what was happening, her first thought was that they were engaged in some kind of feverish contest or game. The girl was Estelle's daughter, Sandra.

"Let's go," Dorothy said, pulling away.

"No," Larry whispered, "let's watch."

"Please," she said, "it's my husband." She turned and blundered back through the bamboo.

Yes, she thought, and I offered to tie his tie, which he still has on. He knows perfectly well how to tie his tie. He said so himself. He was in a highschool play once where he had to tie his tie in front of the audience, as though in front of a mirror: first with one end too long, then with the other one too long, and so on back and forth until finally he got it right. He used to do it at cocktail parties years ago. It looked very funny.

She hurried off across the lawns. In the darker surroundings she could just see the car when Larry caught up with her.

"Wait—don't leave me alone," he said. His voice sounded strange. She herself was in a kind of panic. She grabbed his hand and ran. Now she was the one who was pulling. They got into the car fast, slamming the doors.

She was out on one of the main highways before she remembered what Estelle had told her: that the older married man Sandra had taken on had been Estelle's lover for years.

She sobbed a few times and stepped on the accelerator. Larry heaved himself up over the back seat.

"We're going very fast."

"I'm sorry." She slowed down. As soon as she saw a place to stop, she pulled over to the side.

"I'm all upset. I don't know what to do," she said. Larry disappeared behind the seat again.

"There's a car coming up in back of us."

"It's him," Dorothy shouted. She saw the car in the mirror and recognized Fred, and saw too that he had Sandra with him. "With that girl."

"Do you think he saw me?"

"I don't know." Dorothy stood on the pedal and drove the car screaming out into the road. Three other cars swerved to let her into the stream. People were honking at her.

"I can't let him catch me," she explained. It was really because she didn't want to talk to him, see him, or even think about him at the moment, but as soon as she had spoken, she realized that there was another reason. "If we stop, they'll see you."

"I can kill them for you, and it will be all right."

"No, no, no. It's all right. I just hope the cops aren't out checking."

Fred's car followed. Every dodge Dorothy made was repeated. She thought: and besides, how are we going to get over the border?

"I guess we'll go down by way of the coastline. Then you can swim around to the south and join me."

All at once the rented car shot forward. They were neck and neck now. She looked unsmiling into Sandra's frightened white face. The girl was crying. Next to her, Fred was bent forward over the wheel. He looked tense and desperate. Even from where Dorothy sat, his eyes looked all taken up by the pupils. Larry was sitting straight up. Both the others must have seen him. Fred began to try to run their car off the road.

Dorothy put her foot down harder. She began to pull away. And now Sandra was fighting Fred for the wheel. Suddenly there was a loud crack. Later on, Dorothy found out that it must have been another car behind theirs, which was trying to pass Fred. Behind Dorothy and Larry the two cars hit, parted, crashed and spun, and Fred's car, with Sandra—so it was said afterwards—twisting the wheel, reared up and out over the centre strip and into the traffic coming the other way. To the wild noises of grinding and tearing metal all around her, Dorothy squealed into a skid, travelled for yards, banged the side rail and bounced to a standstill. In the mirror she caught sight of two cars bursting into flames.

"Keep going," Larry said.

"I can't. I'm going to have to leave you here. It's dark. And we're not too far from the sea. Do you think you can make it?"

"I don't like it."

"Neither do I, but that's all there is to it. Remember, we'll meet at the beach. Do you have your sandals with you?"

She kissed him goodbye. Tears ran down her cheeks. He put on his sandals and stepped out of the car, looking both ways. There was no need for caution. Everyone would be looking at the burning wrecks in the road.

Dorothy started the car, drove ahead for a while, looking for a place to turn off, and then realized that she would never be able to get anywhere near Fred's car. That side of the freeway was piling up in a solid mass. Cars were turning off wherever they could, to go in the other direction. If she had stopped to think, she could have kept Larry in the car and driven him back with her. She could even have kept him there at the house. Indefinitely.

Drivers around her were honking their horns at her again. She moved forward, heading for home.

The moment she opened the door, the place felt like a house she had never seen before. It didn't seem to belong to her, or ever have been anyone else's home. It was strange to think that living people could ever have spent their lives in it. The look, the silence—it was so different, so unlike the house where she had moved through so many years of her life, that she thought perhaps if she had only just come in from shopping and not from the scene of the accident, she would have known in any case.

She sat down on a chair and waited. She was home a good three hours before the police telephoned.

When she went to identify the body, Estelle was there in the corridor. She looked like a sleepwalker. She said to Dorothy in a tired whisper, "You've killed me. We kept it from you for years, so you wouldn't be hurt any more. We could have been happy if it hadn't been for you. But you destroy everything around you. Now I'm like you, too. Even my children. That's what you wanted, wasn't it?"

Dorothy shook her head. She said, "It wasn't me," and passed on down the hall. She remembered that at one time, she couldn't now recall just when, Estelle had told her that she, Dorothy, didn't understand the nature of desire. And now she didn't want to understand it, or anything else, either. She had stopped feeling pity and sympathy for other people. One betrayal covered another. She was no longer ready to forgive. Only the note Mr Mendoza put through the door moved her.

Suzanne came to the funeral, of course. She brought her husband and children with her. Dorothy phoned up the doctor and made him say that Suzanne and her family would have to stay in a motel, because to have to cope with in-laws at the house would give Dorothy a nervous breakdown. What was more, her doctor seemed to believe it himself. He was very practical too, and left her with a lot of pills, just enough so that it wouldn't kill her if she took them all at once.

She drove to the beach every night. He never came. She wondered sometimes whether he had seen her begin to drive on back home and thought she had taken the opportunity to get rid of him deliberately. But he couldn't think that, surely not. He would have noticed the traffic. And yet he never came. He couldn't have been captured, or it would have been in the papers and on the news. If he had been hurt or killed, it would be the same. That must mean, then, that there was some reason why he couldn't come. Either he had been hurt in the ocean, perhaps killed, or he was out there, but waiting.

The grave was planted. Dorothy visited it regularly. It was almost her only regular visit. She never saw Estelle, or the Cranstons. Most of the time, she took the telephone off the hook. Her lawyers wrote to her about insurance and inheritance. She looked through the want ads and wrote for interviews. Mr Mendoza went away on his vacation. She ordered the tombstone, and was on nodding acquaintance with an old woman at the cemetery who kept the grave—another new one —next to hers. One day the woman opened up with the story of her husband's life and death.

"Your hubby?" she concluded, pointing to the grave as though it were something she might sell to Dorothy, if pushed. Dorothy nodded. The old woman looked at the place where the headstone would be.

"Some of these long names," she said, "it's hard to fit it all in. Mine was Jim. James. What was yours?"

Dorothy hesitated, confused for a moment. "Fred," she said, and changed her mind, feeling even more confused. "Larry," she added. "His name was actually Frederick. But I called him Larry."

"What was it—his heart?"

"Heart, lungs, head, everything. Car crash."

"Oh, I see," the woman said, losing interest. "An accident."

Dorothy went for two interviews and was told that they would let her know. She wrote a short letter to her parents and told them to stop worrying because it was beginning to make her worry too. She packed up most of Fred's clothes to send to Suzanne, and saved one or two things to give to Mr Mendoza for his cousin in Chicago who ran the shop. She listened to the radio, but there were no special messages now.

She drove down in the evenings to the beach. Sometimes by moonlight and sometimes only by starlight, she stared at the line where the water ran over the sand. He never came. She got out of the car and walked up and down the beach, hour after hour. The water ran over the sand, one wave covering another like the knitting of threads, like the begetting of revenges, betrayals, memories, regrets. And always it made a musical, murmuring sound, a language as definite as speech. But he never came.